# LURE

## TIM McGREGOR

## ILLUSTRATIONS BY KELLY WILLIAMS

*Content warnings are available at the end of this book. Please consult this list for any particular subject matter you may be sensitive to.*

TENEBROUS

PRESS

Production of this novel was made possible in part by a grant from the Regional Arts & Culture Council.
Visit https://racc.org/ for more information.

Published by Tenebrous Press.
Visit our website at www.tenebrouspress.com.

First Printing, July 2022.

ISBN: 978-1-7379823-0-2
eBook ISBN: 978-1-7379823-1-9

Cover illustration by Matt Blairstone.

Interior illustrations by Kelly Williams.

Edited by Alex Woodroe and Matt Blairstone.

Formatting by Lori Michelle.

Printed in the United States of America.

# 1

THE SEA MONSTER measures forty-six hands across. Its bones hang on the wall in our church, spanning the length of the chancel. According to legend, it is over nine hundred years old. The tail is enormous, like that of some titanic serpent, but the fore end is a hodgepodge of mismatched anatomy. The skull is human, as are the ribs and arms, but there is also the dried baleen of a whale and the bill of a swordfish incorporated into its frame. It is ghastly looking, but impressive.

It's also very dusty.

"When was the last time this relic was cleaned, do you suppose?" my father says. It is his church now. He is the Reverend Uriah Lensman, pastor here for the last five years.

Father cranes his long neck to look up at the garish relic suspended on the stone wall, a good three fathoms above the floor, blackened with soot from a thousand years of burning candles. It hovers above the icon of our holy creator, the One True God. As far as I know, ours is the only church in the realm to shelter the bones of a monster.

"I don't think it's ever been cleaned," I reply. "The damned thing is so old it might fall apart if I try dusting it."

"Language, Kaspar, please," he sighs. "Here of all places."

An old complaint. My mouth often runs faster than my brains. "Sorry, father."

My name is Kaspar Lensman. I am fifteen years. My sister, Bryndis, is seventeen. Pip is eleven, and his nose has never stopped running. His full name is Pitr, but no one calls him that. Mother is dead.

Father lays a ribbon to mark his place and closes the parish registry. Yesterday's birth has been added to the ledger. Another boy. "Fetch the ladder," he says. "See what you can do about it. Have you been down to the pier yet?"

"No. The fishermen won't be back yet."

"Well, don't wait to long," he grumbles. "You need to be there when they return, otherwise they'll cheat us out of our supper."

The pier is the last place I want to go. It's not even my duty to perform, but Father insists he is too busy to collect the tithe from the townsfolk. Liar. "Yes, sir."

Father steps away and crosses to the side door that leads to the rectory, where we live. "Leandra said her husband netted a seal pup yesterday. What I wouldn't give for a taste of red meat. Or anything besides codfish."

"I thought it was bad luck to eat seal."

"Says the man who fails to catch one," he replies as he goes out the door. The Reverend Uriah thinks of himself as a man of high wit, but I have yet to hear anyone laugh at his quips. He believes this is because of his intellect and education, but in truth, he is simply a humorless, taciturn man. A man of the true faith, not of the people, as he often reminds me.

The ladder is a wobbly thing that looks as old as the church itself. Climbing up, I pray it doesn't snap under me as I dab the bones with a damp rag. Up close, I can see how the sea monster is constructed; the various bones are lashed together with twine or fastened with penny nails. A patchwork of misaligned bone and tooth, fused together to form this bizarre holy relic.

How in the world did the carcass of a monster come to hang inside the church? The story, as it's been told to me, hearkens back to the very founding of this village here on the craggy coast. A long, long time ago, this squalid settlement was bedeviled by a monster from the sea depths. It snatched men from their skiffs and slithered ashore to devour women and children in their sod huts. It ravaged the goats and swallowed horses whole. The old wives claimed that the beast, having had a taste of warm blood with that first unlucky fisherman, wanted no more cold fish from the sea. It lusted then for the creatures of dry land, especially those that strode on two legs.

The peasant folk prayed to the old gods of the sea to save them, but they were dead and could not hear their cries. In desperation, some turned their backs on the old ways and lifted their prayers to the heavens and to the sun and to whatever could hear them. Behold, one soul, one righteous heart, heard their lamentations and came riding out of the mountain in the sky on a great steed that blew flames from its nostrils. A hero named Torgrim the Unbending, holding high a sword forged in the furnace of the sun itself. Its steel was lit with holy fire and it thirsted hungrily for the blood of the wicked and the heathen alike. The hero charged his horse through the sea foam and dared the monster to challenge him. The sea churned and chopped, and the great serpent lunged for the man who dared defy it. Torgrim the Unbending smote the beast with his flaming sword, cleaving the monster in two. The beast writhed on the pebbly beach, smoking from the holy flame as the blade drank its blood. The grateful pagans lifted the hero on their shoulders, proclaimed him king, and adopted his faith of the one true God.

Or so the legend tells. I laughed when I first heard the tale, which did not endear me to the locals. A gaffe, which only caused the villagers to dislike us even more when my father became pastor to this far-flung parish. Half the people in the village claim to be direct descendants of this noble hero, which explains the number of men named Torgu or the daughters named Torga.

I am the only Kaspar in town. Most snicker at my name behind my back. A few do it to my face. Fitting in has not been easy. We will always be outsiders, my family and I.

The sea monster measures forty-six hands across. Its bones hang on the wall in our church, spanning the length of the chancel. According to legend, it is over nine hundred years old.

# 2

BEFORE HEADING TO the pier to collect the tithe, I decide to check my own traps. With any luck there will be a crab or maybe a few cod, which will allow me to skip the tithing altogether. I hate having to beg the fishermen. And they hate me for it in return.

A set of worn stone steps lead down to the church crypt, where the former reverends and the prominent men of the village are interred. The stone walls here are cold and always damp with saltwater. The church was built on the cliffside over the sea, with the crypt chiseled out of the rock. Another passageway leads from the tombs down to a wooden hut on the sea. My traps are tethered here, strung down into the dark water, and baited with a few dinner scraps.

Hauling both traps out of the water proves disappointing. The bait is gone, but no crabs or fish have been captured. These creatures are wily, having figured out how to nip the bait without being snared. I throw the traps back into the water and climb the stairs to the church. I have no choice but to go begging for the tithe now.

The church sits high on the escarpment, overlooking the village. From here, all one sees are the battered roofs of the cottages clustered before the enclosed bay. Beyond that, open sea. The mountain range that rings our little village is treacherous to pass, closing us off from the rest of the world. The only way in or out of Torgrimsvær is by sea.

Life here on the razor's edge of the known world is difficult. Here the stars twinkle green at night and the sun turns a rich blood red at midday. It is not a place for the weak, and the people of this northern coast are a proud lot. Hardy and resilient, they proclaim themselves God's chosen people, and thus, superior to those in other realms. The kingdoms of the east they consider to be degenerate, and the empires in the south are flabby and weak. Westerners are devils incarnate. The Almighty favors those whose flesh is hardened by salty winds and hard toil.

The village square is small, but it contains a stone fountain built over the very spot where it is said Torgrim the Unbending slew the great sea monster. I'm told villagers used to toss pennies into it as a wishing well, back when the fishing was plentiful. People hold onto their pennies now. The coins are long gone, taken by the village boys who dove in to fetch them from the bottom of the fountain. All those wishes, stolen by naked, shivering boys. The fountain has since evaporated to a few feet of brackish water that smells badly. No one makes wishes anymore.

My father was assigned to this remote coastal parish when I was ten years old. We packed our paltry belongings and made the long sail to this desolate fishing village hidden away from the rest of the world. Mother did not want to go. She was a country girl with soil under her fingernails and hay in her hair. She had no wish to trade our small farm for a hut on the bitter coast. My father assured her that being granted his own parish was a great advancement for himself and our family. Prestige, prominence and comfort, he promised. None of this materialized. There is barely a speck of greenery in this place. It is rock and mountains and the sea. Grey and cold.

Three years after settling in Torgrimsvær, Mother vanished. No one really knows what happened to her, but local tongues like to wag. They claim that, unable to bear her unhappiness, Mother filled her pockets with stones and stepped off the pier.

One benefit of becoming the new reverend, my father was

assured, was that the fishermen were duty bound to provide for their spiritual leader. Father had envisioned the men happily bringing us the catch of the day, the women offering bread from their own kilns, but this was not the case. Father had to go down to the pier and ask the fishermen for whatever they could spare, which the men would comply with the smallest or sickliest of the day's catch. The tithe, they sneered. It was humiliating, my father would complain to mother at the dinner table. In time, he refused to do it, sending me in his stead.

It is the worst part of my day, going round hat in hand like a beggar. Agrippa, sitting in his little skiff, offers up a minnow no larger than a finger. Otho's tithe is a single clam. Wall-eyed Wilfrid has nothing at all, holding up his empty net to show me.

"I'm sorry, Kaspar," he says, his left eye rolling east. "Luck was not with me today."

"Not a single fish, Wilfrid? How will your family eat?" Wilfrid and his goodwife have seven children. All are thinner than spiders, but they have the appetites of lions.

His smile is contrite. "The missus is a sorceress at the stove. She can always conjure something for us to sup on."

I watch the poor man sway in his little boat and feel pity for him. I reach into my basket for a fish. "Today's tithing is slim, but I could spare this minnow. Take it."

His coarse-calloused hand waves the notion away. "No, no. I'll not have our reverend go hungry. Tomorrow, God willing, will be a better day."

"I pray it is. Good day, Wilf."

The offerings from the other men are equally stingy. The catch in my basket is barely enough to feed a cat. Another night when the family shall go to bed hungry.

The last boat is docked at the far end of the quay, away from the others. A trim sloop with a single mast and a maiden carved into the prow. The skipper of this vessel is Gunther Torgmundsin, a scarred giant of a man. Gunther the Brave, as he is called. Like most villagers, Gunther claims to be a descendant of the fabled hero that slew the sea monster. In Gunther's case, it is probably true. His arms are thicker than tree trunks and laced with white scars from his years of hunting fish. He used to be a harpooner on whaling ships, spearing the leviathans with his weapon, and riding the beasts down. His tales are legendary.

When Gunther the Brave sees me coming, his face breaks into a grin. "Well, well. If it isn't the little beggar boy."

"How was the fishing today, Gunther? Was the sea good to you?"

"The sea was a proper bitch this day." Reaching into his nets, he holds up two creatures that barely resemble fish at all. "Or she was having a joke on me. I can't decide."

One creature is armored, like a lobster. It looks more like an insect than a fish. The other is a ball with spikes.

"What are they?"

"God only knows," he says. "But boiled and salted, I'm sure they'll taste fine."

I nod at the spiked thing. "Isn't that one poisonous?"

"Only to the weak," he laughs and tosses the damned thing into my basket. There is a scar on Gunther's face, livid and white, that runs from his brow to his jawline. A swordfish off the Borsican coast had tried to pluck out his eye. Its sailfin now decorates the hearth in his cottage.

"Mind the pointy bits when you fillet that," he adds. "But be sure to get the heart. It's the tastiest morsel on the whole thing."

"Thank you, Gunther."

"How is the Reverend? The family?"

"Fine." I look at the meager bounty in the basket. "Grateful, as always."

The scar on Gunther's face crinkles when he speaks. "Be content with what you have, son. God may choose to wash us into the sea tomorrow."

This is a common saying in our village. It baffled me

when we settled here. It's meant to remind everyone to be humble in their position and to never tempt fate by puffing oneself up like the morning rooster. When asked how one is faring, the answer is always 'fine' or 'well enough'. To say one is happy is considered boastful, which risks having it all swept away. Few people smile in our village.

"Tell your father to fasten the shutters tonight," the giant fisherman says. He wags his chin north, where the sky is darkening. "There's a squall coming in."

Thanking him again, I leave Gunther to his nets and head home with the dismal catch for our dinner. Halfway down the stone pier, I see Agnet coming the other way. I could no more stop the smile on my face than I could stop the sun from going down. I don't see much of Agnet Guiscard these days. Not since last summer, anyway.

"Hello Kaspar," she says, risking a smile. "Has the sea been good to you?"

Agnet is sixteen. A year older than I am. Not everyone would agree that Agnet is the prettiest girl in our village, but those people are fools. Or blind. Or possibly insane. Her eyes are brown and as big as pennies, but there is a light to them that I have seen in no other. She has freckles everywhere.

"Well enough," I reply, letting her peek into the frayed basket.

"The fish are being coy with everyone these days," she says. Her nose wrinkles. "What is that spiky thing? Is it even a fish?"

"I'll find out when I scale it." I feel my face grinning like the village idiot's. "You look well. How is your mother? Doing better, I hope."

The light in her eyes dims a little. "She's still abed. I pray she'll recover, but I don't think my prayers are worth much."

"I'm sorry. That must be very hard, looking after her as well as keeping your other, uh, duties."

"I am content with it. God may wash us all out to sea tomorrow."

9

That damn admonition again. It floats everywhere here, dripping from the slate roofs and rolling along the cobblestones. There's no escaping it.

"If there's anything I can do to help, Agnet. Sit with your mother or fetch peat for the fire. Anything."

"That's kind of you," she says. The breeze ripples up from the sea and blows her hair over her eyes. When Agnet smiles, she reveals a wide gap between her front teeth. She's overly mindful of it, but it is her best feature. She's about to say something when a voice bellows along the quay for her to quit dawdling.

"Goodbye, Kaspar."

Gathering her skirts, she hurries along the pier to the vessel at the far end, where Gunther is hollering for her. Her husband these last twelve months. They married a fortnight before Midsummer when the fishing was plentiful.

# 3

"**I**S THIS A JOKE?" asks my sister. "What am I to do with this?"

She grimaces at the paltry contents of the basket. I shrug. "This is what they had."

"Father won't be happy with this."

"Is there anything he's happy with?" I take the sharpest knife in the kitchen to clean the fish. "Where is Father?"

"In the church," Bryndis says. "Sligo came to see him. He said it was urgent."

"What was so urgent?"

I square my sister with a look. This could be bad news, but she dismisses my alarm. "He didn't say," she says.

Bryndis dabs a wrist against her brow. It is washing day, and she's been toiling over a hot cauldron all afternoon, scrubbing and wringing our garments. Bryndis is seventeen, the oldest sibling. She has our mother's dark hair and impudent nose. Mother claimed that her family was descended from eastern royalty, exiled here to the north because of some palace intrigue. I do not know if this is true, but she fervently believed it. Bryndis, I think, wants to believe this claim, also. She certainly acts regal in the way that she orders my brother and I about. Since Mother's disappearance, Bryndis has taken on more of a parental role in our home. Or that role was yoked around her neck by default.

I gather up the basket again. "Let me clean these. Hopefully, there's enough to make a stew out of."

"You need to cook tonight," she says, nodding to the heap of washing left to do.

Glancing over to the kitchen, I do not see our brother. "Why isn't Pip helping you?"

"He's having one of his fits." Her eyes dart to the pantry.

Pulling back the curtain, I find Pip on the pantry floor. My brother looks ill, but in all honesty, he's looked sick since the day he was born. He lifts his head, all red-rimmed eyes and running nose. Pale skin and thin limbs, but an oddly rounded belly. Not a stitch of clothing on him.

"Where are your clothes?"

"It's too hot in here," he says.

"You'll catch your death, you little idiot." Mind you, if Pip caught a cold, none of us would know the difference. "Get dressed and help your sister."

He shrieks. A long, sustained note of ear-piercing pitch that does not stop until I draw the pantry curtain closed.

I augur a finger into my ear to relieve the pain and look at Bryndis. "One of those days, I see."

A noise from the yard has Bryndis and me looking up. Father and Sligo are saying goodbye. Sligo, with his absurdly long arms and bulbous nose, makes a point to doff his cap to Bryndis before he goes out the gate. Father scowls to see us gawking from the kitchen.

"Bryndis, come here," he says. "We must talk."

My sister is abruptly pale. Her jaw clenches as she grits her teeth at what is to come. Then she lowers her head and does what she is told.

***

The cutting block in the yard is a prehistoric tree stump tempered dark from the countless fish cleaned on it. Scales dot the surface, twinkling in the waning sunlight. Our home, the rectory, is set back from the church and screened behind a hedge. I slit the blackfish up the belly, mindful of its spikes, and remove its entrails. There is not a lot of meat on this stingy little fish.

The slam of a door lifts my attention and I see my sister march into the yard in tears. She flops onto a log and buries her face in her hands. The bad news she has been dreading is here.

"I'm sorry," I tell her. Little comfort, that is. "Who is it to be?"

She drags a sleeve across her nose. "Sligo."

At seventeen, Bryndis has managed to elude the fate of most girls in the village. No longer, the ax has fallen. Sligo has asked for her hand in marriage and Father consented. It is the way of things here. Sligo's wife died this winter. Gerda had drowned in two feet of water in the old fountain. As a widower, it is Sligo's privilege to choose any girl in the village for his bride. As a member of the council, it's his right not to be refused. Father has no choice but to consent.

"I'm sorry, Bryn." I don't know what else to say by way of condolence.

My sister is level-headed and even-tempered. Already she is drying her eyes. She looks at me.

"What am I to tell Calder?"

Her sweetheart. Calder is a year older than Bryndis, a fisherman's son who lives near the wharf. He is almost as penniless as we are. I like Calder. He has always been kind to me.

"The truth," I say. "He'll understand. He'll have to."

***

The stew turns out awful. A sour gruel with a strange taste that must have come from the blackfish. Bryndis grimaces while slurping it down and Pip won't touch it, but Pip rarely eats anything at all. He sits slouched in his chair with his nose running into his soup.

"Pip, wipe your nose," my sister says with annoyance.

Pip continues to stare at the wall in that absent way of his. He startles when I kick him under the table, and then stirs the spoon in his bowl.

Father sits at the head of the table, lapping his stew up

without comment. His eyes are on the open book before him. He only looks up to scold us to be quiet. Mealtimes are like this, these grim and silent affairs. It wasn't always this way.

Bryndis is tired, her hands raw from the day's toil. She is heartbroken but hides it. Pip sits as thoughtless as a turnip. I remark how paltry the tithe from the fishermen is, but everyone has heard this complaint already. The Reverend Uriah continues to read and loudly slurp up his stew. Does he even taste it?

Our small family is four in number, but a fifth place is always set at our table. An empty plate and the good spoon, the pewter one. Pip was the one who insisted we set a place for Mother in case she returns. My sister and I went along with it to keep him happy. We have tried to shield him from the gossip about mother's disappearance as much as possible. Pip has been setting this fifth, empty plate for so long that it is simply routine, and we take little notice of it anymore.

Pip sometimes brings it up. He is absentminded, with a potato-shaped head that leaks things. He snaps out of his blank stare, sees the empty place setting, and asks when Mother is coming home. No one responds, eyes on our plates, and then Pip will remember and fall silent again.

That first winter after she vanished, the three of us would tell one another stories about where she had gone. Pip said she had been snatched away by an albatross and dropped into a volcano where she lives with a family of giants. Bryndis spun a tale where Mother was swallowed by a whale. I preferred a story about the sea god, Nomos, sweeping her off to his undersea kingdom to be queen for one year. At the end of her reign, she will return with treasure chests gathered from sunken ships as her reward. Pip once asked if Mother prefers her undersea home now and that is why she hasn't returned to us. Bryndis fled the room in tears hearing that.

They were just fairy tales told to comfort and distract. Come spring that year, we stopped telling them. Pip, to this day, will try to entice us into retelling our stories, but neither Bryndis nor I have the stomach for it. Sometimes Pip recites the fairy tales to himself, sitting out on the cutting block in the yard, talking to the air.

"Pip, wake up."

He has fallen asleep. He does this more and more these days, falling asleep while sitting up. Eyes half-closed, nose running. It is disturbing.

Father looks up from his book. "Pitr," he says, snapping the boy awake. "Eat."

Pip spoons the fish broth into his mouth and makes a strange clucking sound as he eats. He drops the spoon and claps his hands. "It's Midsummer Eve!" he cries.

Father scowls but keeps his eyes on his book.

"Can we wrestle an octopus?" Pip asks. "Or roast a shark?"

"No more talking," Father replies. "Eat."

The good Reverend Uriah never liked the Midsummer Eve festivities here. Too pagan and too bawdy, he complained. He despised the vulgar rituals that honored the old sea gods and frowned on the tradition of the merry husbands who chose a different wife for the shortest night of the year. Last year, he forbade them outright, and so the day passes like any other. A little more sunlight, but that is all.

Outside, the wind has picked up, rattling the precious glass in the window. I suddenly remember the warning from Agnet's husband.

"There's a storm coming."

Father's eyes never stray from his book. "It's just the wind, Kaspar."

"Gunther says it's going to be a squall."

The book is closed, my father out of his chair. A weather warning from the hero harpooner is not to be taken lightly.

"On your feet, all of you," Father says. "We need to seal the shutters before it lands."

# 4

THE RAIN HITS before we seal all the windows. It comes down in a torrent that blinds us as we latch the shutters in the church. It's whipped along by a wind so powerful it sweeps Pip, who weighs no more than a barncat, off his feet and sends him tumbling through the headstones in the churchyard. It is not necessarily a bad thing in his case, as Pip is always filthy. He refuses to bathe. The best any of us can manage is to toss a penny into the surf and make him fetch it.

We are all drenched and steaming and very tired when we go up to bed. Father has the only proper bedroom in the house. It has a window that looks out onto the sea. The three of us share the rest of the space with cots lined up against the trunks and crates. Bryndis has fashioned a screen over her corner to provide a little privacy.

Father snores the loudest, great thunder strokes cracking behind the bedroom door. My sister sounds like a cat. Pip sings in his sleep. Mostly sea shanties, the vulgar kind that the fishermen sing when deep in their cups.

We peel out of our steaming clothes and hang them to dry on the railing. We say our prayers in the light of the candle. It is Pip's turn to lead the prayer, and he prattles on, thanking the Almighty for our home and our food and each other. Then he goes on, grateful for stray kittens and seashells, termite hills and starfish. When he mentions toadstools and earwax, Bryndis interrupts.

"That's enough. Just say Amen."

"But I haven't mentioned the sea monster's bones."

"God knows you're grateful for that. Into bed."

The wind whips at the house, tearing at the roof and rattling the doors. There aren't enough pots to catch the rainwater leaking from the rafters. My brother thrusts out his tongue to catch the raindrops until our sisters tells him to stop.

"I want a story."

"Not tonight, Pip," Bryndis says. She looks tired.

"Just one. The one about the pirates."

I push his head to the pillow. "Listen to your sister."

He frowns. "I can't remember how mother told it. Was it pirates or lepers? The ones on the bottom of the sea? You remember."

Some of Mother's bedtime stories took strange turns. This particular one was a favorite of Pip's, an odd fable about the fate of pirates and how they are condemned to walk the floor of the sea to atone for their sins. They march in a never-ending parade until their feet are ground away by the sand, and they marched onward on bony stumps. Was it the fate of pirates or cruel men? I can't remember. Is there a difference?

I pat my brother's bulbous head. "Go to sleep now."

He frowns, but closes his eyes. Bryn slips behind her screen to change into her nightshirt. In the pocket of my jacket are three daisies plucked from the hillside. They are soggy and most of the petals have fallen away. I set them out gently under my pillow.

My sister steps out from behind the screen, her brow crinkling. "What are you doing?"

"You put flowers under your pillow on Midsummer's Eve to dream about the one you love," I explain.

"You can't do that, Kaspar."

My sister and her rules. So bossy. "Why not?"

"Only girls put flowers under their pillows at Midsummer."

"What do boys put under pillows?"

"They don't," she says with a huff. "It's not natural."

"I'm doing it, anyway."

I lay the pillow over the soggy daisies and climb into bed. Pip is already asleep and singing his sea shanties. This one is about a sailor who falls in love with an oyster and loses his pizzle on his wedding night.

I watch my sister take something from the pocket of her apron and arrange it under her pillow.

"Daisies?" I ask. "To dream about Calder?"

She holds an object up to the light. A fishhook.

I'm confused. "What kind of dreams do fishhooks bring?"

"No dreams," she says as she lays her head down. "Fishhooks snare wedding vows, killing them."

Her intended marriage to the great oaf, Sligo. I have not heard of this fishhook trick to spoil a marriage, but I admire my sister's craftiness.

I blow out the candle. "I hope it works."

"Goodnight, Kaspar."

Pip sings his shanty, getting to the part where the severed manhood is polished into a pearl inside the oyster's shell. When he finally dozes off, I hear my sister crying herself to sleep.

***

The storm is a rough one, with a wind that keeps us awake as it clatters the door and whistles down the chimney. The shutters hold, the windows survive. By morning, it is all over and the sun rises strong on the rain-drenched village. A boat moored on the pier has capsized and some of the cottages have lost a window or swaths of thatch from their roofs. Fish have been swept up out of the sea and flung right into the town square. I watch a crab scuttling over the roof of the blacksmith's shop.

The three of us are clearing storm debris from our yard, when Pip finds a starfish under the hedge. Bryndis tells him to toss it back into the sea, but Pip wants to keep it for a pet.

"Don't be stupid," I tell him. "You can't make a pet out of that."

"Why not? A starfish would be the perfect pet. I'm going to name him Goblin."

Pip runs to fill a pail from the rain barrel and places the creature in it. Freshwater, not sea water. The thing is dead within the hour.

"Poor Goblin," he sighs, looking into the pail.

Everyone in the village is up and about by this time, sweeping up the mess left behind by the storm. The sun is bright, and neighbors wish one another a good morning. They chatter about the ferocity of the winds and how no one slept a wink.

A sudden clamor hails out on the pier and we look up to see a fisherman running about, howling his fool head off. There is something in the water, he screams. He saw it with his own eyes, God help him.

Pip holds the dead starfish in his hand. It is already beginning to stink. "What is he screaming about?"

Bryndis shrugs. "He says there's something in the bay."

The crazed fisherman is repeating one word over and over, and I crane my ear to catch it. "He says he saw a luremaid in the harbor."

Bryndis shields her eyes from the sun. "Is he drunk?"

Pip's face pinches. "What's a luremaid?"

My sister laughs. "A mermaid."

# 5

THE SAILOR ISN'T DRUNK, and he isn't delusional. Out there, far into the bay, is a woman bobbing on the sea.

The three of us run to the wharf. Everyone in the village has the same idea, and we all elbow one another for a closer look.

"Did someone fall in?" says a woman on my left.

"Who is it?" croaks an old man on my right. "Is it my Lilja? She can't swim."

"God help her, she won't last another minute in that cold."

Whoever uttered that is right. Even in high summer, the water is freezing. And yet the woman out there in the bay does not appear distressed or drowning. She hovers on the ripples for a moment and then we all gasp as she slips below the waves. Agrippa and Bjarni have already launched their boats, rowing like mad toward the damsel's position.

A boy cries out, points. "Look, there!"

And there she is, two leagues from where she'd gone under. No one can swim that fast. The waves dapple the sunlight back at us in blinding flashes. It must have tricked our eyes.

The briny sailor who started all the fuss is still shrieking about a mermaid. Someone tries to calm him, but he shoves them away and leaps into his dory.

"I'll catch her!" he sings, dipping his oars into the water. "She'll make a pretty wife!"

Shielding my eyes from the sun, I scan the bay but cannot locate the drowning woman. I look to Bryndis. "Where did she go?"

"She went under again. Dear God, preserve the poor woman."

Someone else shouts and points and we all turn to see a head bob to the surface. Much closer to the pier this time. A pale face with dark locks. Is her hair really green or is it another trick of the light?

She swims toward us, and every voice dies as she cuts the dark water, moving with an undulating rhythm not unlike that of a whale. That's when we see it, all of us popping our eyes in disbelief. The tail. Enormous and long, more like that of a serpent than a fish. Hand over my heart, the woman has a tail where her legs should be.

Someone utters a prayer. An old man drops to his knees and weeps. The woman in the water, this mermaid of fairy tales, watches us with cold eyes as she glides along the length of the wharf. Then she dives, that great tail arcing as it breaks the surface of the water. She is gone. *It* is gone, whatever it is.

The townsfolk shake their heads and rub their eyes as if waking from a dream. Calamity immediately follows. People shout and run about. The women race for dry land, herding their children before them, while the men all scramble to their skiffs. Nets are readied, harpoons raised, as they all row out into the bay. In the eyes of each man is a mad look as they prepare to hunt the thing they have seen. Something about this creature has them gnashing their teeth, driving them on to spear this fabled luremaid of the depths. Her brazen freedom offends them somehow.

One sloop remains tethered to the dock. Gunther's fine vessel. The skipper is roaring at a boy on the pier, demanding to know where Brom is. His fishing mate and oarsmen. The boy crushes his hat in his hand and explains that his father is unwell.

"You mean drunk!" Gunther bellows.

His face is red as he stomps the hull of his boat. The boy jumps and quivers all the more. The scarred harpooner casts his eyes about the chaos on the quay and, of all people, locks onto me.

"Kaspar! Get in the boat! Now!"

I shake my head vigorously. "I'm no whaler."

"I don't need a whaler, lad. I need someone to row!"

His powerful arm shoots out and plants me onto the slat bench of his boat. Row, he insists. So I row.

"Faster, lad," Gunther howls as he lashes the end of the spooled rope to his great harpoon. "Starboard now! That's it."

The bay becomes a choppy stew of boats and yammering fishermen, each chasing this thing from a storybook tale. Nets are spun into the waves and harpoons fly and miss. To a man, they all seem crazed with the idea of spearing this fabled creature of the depths. An armada of madmen, fishing for folk tales.

I catch only a glimpse of the woman in the water. Astern, her head bobs for a moment, only to appear a heartbeat later on the port side. She eludes the spears and nets like it's a game.

Gunther keeps barking directions at me. Port five degrees, he says. Starboard now, ten degrees. Twenty. I twist about to see where he is aiming and catch sight of the woman in the water. Gunther is tracking the creature's movements, closing the distance quickly. The harpoon in his hand rises high, ready to strike.

"Double knots now!" he growls. "Row, boy! Row like your soul's at stake!"

I see him throw just as the mermaid breaks the surface again. The needle strikes its target, and the strange fish-woman spins around and around in the water, churning the waves into foam with her fury. Ulric, in the nearest skiff, casts his net, only to see it twist around the thrashing thing.

The tether rope on the harpoon unspools crazily out of the boat as its target swims away. The boat pitches forward violently, washing waves into the hull. Gunther almost crushes me in his fall. The man weighs a bloody ton.

"The chase is on!" Gunther cries as the vessel skims the waves, pulled along at frightening speed by the thing he has speared. Dry land vanishes behind us fast and I become seasick. The chop pounds the hull so hard I fear the boat will split apart.

In a flash, it is over. The line snaps and the boat settles into a gentle bob. Gunther roars a string of obscenities that hovers over the bay while I lurch over the stern to spill my stomach into the sea.

I wipe my mouth and look across to the skipper. Gunther sits on the gunwale, lighting his long-stemmed pipe. The leering grin on his scarred face makes me turn green all over again.

"Damndest thing I ever saw," he says. He flings the match out to sea and regards me for a long moment with the smoke billowing across his face. Taking the pipe from his teeth, he points the stem at me. "Valiant effort, Kaspar. You're stronger than you look. You can be my oarsman any day."

When I retch a second time, he laughs and orders me to lay down and be still. Clamping the pipe in his teeth, he takes the oars and rows for home.

\*\*\*

Gunther is given a hero's welcome when we dock, the other fishermen clapping him on the back and praising the strength of his arm. Questions buzz through the crowd like blowflies on a carcass. Did Gunther kill the creature? Is it truly a mermaid? Where did it come from? Why is it here?

I crawl out of the boat and collapse like a dirty dishclout on the stone pier, still green around the gills. The throng moves on, circling their hero.

One person stops to ask if I am all right. Agnet, of course. She bends low to flatten a palm over my brow.

"That was quite the ride it gave you," she says. "Are you going to be sick?"

Humiliated, I wave her concern away. "It'll pass. Sorry."

Agnet smiles, revealing the gap between her teeth. Overly conscious of it her whole life, Agnet has taught herself to smile close-mouthed. But not with me. I miss seeing that dark space.

"You need to find your sea legs, Kaspar."

I snort up a laugh. An old joke between us. For someone who lives on the sea, I do not like the water. "I forgot them up at the house."

She takes in the expanse of the bay that protects our hamlet from the harsher open water. "Did you get a good look at it?"

"No more than a glimpse. It was fast."

Her brow knits into a curious crease. "Is it really what they say it is? It wasn't a dolphin or a seal?"

"It was real," I say, rising on unsteady legs. "I swear to God, it was real."

Her eyes go back to the waves. "Where in the world did it come from?"

There is no answer to this question, so I do not respond. An awkwardness settles over me like a frost.

"Maybe I'll catch it in one of my traps."

"Are you still running those out of the hut?"

I nod. "It gives me an excuse to go there."

Her smile drops away and she won't look me in the eyes, now. I despise my own neediness.

"You'll have a little competition to catch her." She nods to where a dozen boys and old men have lined up along the quay to cast lines into the water. Some have baited their hooks with scraps of fish or small mice, but the old man nearest to us ties a silver ring to his hook.

Agnet asks him what it is and we trade sneaky glances when he tells us it is a wedding band. The luremaid, he says, is here to claim a husband to whisk away to her home

24

beneath the waves. Bouncing the wedding band on its string, he grins and says: "How else does one bait a mermaid?"

We giggle at this until a voice bellows over the heads of the fishermen and quashes the mirth. A cable in Agnet's neck tightens briefly at the sound of her husband's voice.

"Duty calls," she says in a clenched, irritated tone. The light in her eyes goes flat like a snuffed candle wick. She walks away, head down.

Bryndis and Pip find me and say it's time to go home. Bryndis asks what I saw out there in the boat and Pip races ahead. He wants to be the one to tell father about the mermaid. When we get to the church, I tell my sister I am going to check my traps. Down to the crypt and down the dank passageway to the sea and the brittle wooden shack built over the rocks.

I don't bother with the traps. I just wanted to come down here. Memories linger in this shed, trapped in the cobwebs of the rafters and the brine-bleached floor.

A spool of rope sits near the hatchway that opens onto the sea. The rope has sat untouched for so long that a dipper has built a nest of mud and twigs on it. It's empty now, the hatchlings raised and flown off. I tug the spool and slide it away to see what's hidden beneath it. Letters, whittled into the wooden floorboards, circled by a crudely carved heart. This is what it says:

*Agnet + Kaspar*

We used to sneak down here all the time to languish on the bed of loose netting and whisper secrets into one another's ears. We would curl up on the floor and look out at the open sea while the breeze cooled our skin. Agnet was the first friend I made when we moved here. Father was aghast when he learned that the village of Torgrimsvær had no school. He started one immediately, but it only lasted a fortnight before he threw his hands up and declared the children unteachable. Agnet had been one of the few pupils to attend the school. She sat next to me on the bench that first day, flashing the gap between her front teeth. She had a fossil that she said brought good luck. I showed her the copper I always kept in my pocket for the same reason. We traded charms that day, promising to keep each other's treasure safe. I kept hers under my pillow until Pip found it and used the fossil to smash snails in the garden. I don't know if Agnet still has the coin. Perhaps she had to spend it.

Friendship became something more. Skinned knees gave way to flustered first kisses. We traded vows, with no one to witness them, that we would find a cottage somewhere, anywhere, and be happy. Since the age of twelve, I have saved every penny I could earn, swindle, or beg for that glorious day. It hasn't added up to much, hard currency being hard to come by, but it was a goal. A childish, silly one, it turns out.

Two winters ago, Gunther the Brave lost his wife. Isolde had fallen ill with some wasting ailment and was gone within a month. Gunther mourned for the appropriate time and then began looking for a new wife. Agnet's father owed the burly fisherman a debt, and when Agnet turned fifteen, Gunther came to collect. She lowered her head, and her pretty tooth-gap was seen no more.

This morning's adventure, being Gunther's oarsman, was a bitter twist to it all. Funny now, to think of becoming second-mate on his fishing boat. It's not all bitter, I suppose. At least I got to see Agnet for a short time. She is usually trapped inside Gunther's little cottage. The feel of her fingertips on my brow has broken something inside me. Looking at our initials carved in the floor is brine to a sucking flesh wound. I slide the rope back to hide it.

Under the floor, I hear the water lap and crash on the rocks. But there is another sound, odd and out of place. An outlandish, plaintive noise.

The water is cold on my shins as I climb down to see what's under the fishing hut. All I see is a scaly hide, enormous and coiled in the tight space between rock and shed. And then I see her face, and the netting tangled tight over the mermaid's flukes.

# 6

I GAPE STUPIDLY at it, my brain trying to catch up with what my eyes are seeing. The thing we had chased in the harbor is coiled up under the hut, tangled in netting and bleeding from the harpoon strike. It flinches at my appearance, recoiling further into the cramped space between the wooden structure and the rocks. The tail is enormous in length, the scales iridescent in this light. Pale skin and hair the color of kelp. The fingers are webbed, the eyes dark and locked right on me.

I should run. I should scream for help and bring the entire village down to see what I've found, but I don't. My brain flops this way and that, trying to simply comprehend this creature, this luremaid.

Both of my hands go up, palms exposed. "I do not mean you any harm."

It does not reply, of course. It flinches at the sound of my voice and retreats further into the tight space. Did I really expect it to speak the same language? Or even understand me?

It is clearly hurt. There's blood everywhere and the wound in her ribs is raw and gaping. The tail is tangled in the fisherman's net so tight that it cuts into the scaly flesh. It grimaces each time it moves, the net cutting deeper. Tangled thus, it cannot swim. I'm surprised the creature made it this far.

I'm unsure what to do, snared between an urge to run to Father and another, contradictory urge to help this beast.

28

The outcome of the former makes me shudder, so I choose the latter. I slip the knife from my belt. When I move closer, the creature hisses at me. It is an awful sound.

I coo at it, the way one approaches a wild animal or a violent drunk. I promise not to hurt it, I tell it everything will be all right. The mermaid keeps hissing until I cut away the first threads of the netting. It settles, still wary, but not thwarting my attempt to saw through the fishing net. The hemp has sliced deep into the scales and blood runs as I peel it away. I avoid looking directly into its dark eyes, afraid I might provoke it. When the cutting is done, I gently tug the last of the cruel netting away and she is free.

A degree of hardness melts from her features. She seems suddenly spent and exhausted now that the net is gone. The strange gills on her neck fan open and close with the regularity of a heartbeat. The eyes close.

Will it survive and swim away or will it die here in this cramped space under the fishing hut? Maybe my father could hang her bones inside the church, a companion to the original? Are the two, in fact, related?

Too many questions for too empty a head as mine to puzzle out. I will let the thing rest and return in the morning. No one else need know of its existence. I will leave her fate in God's hands.

Before leaving, I check my trap lines. To my delight, I find a large crab snared in one of the cages. Enough to feed all of us, enough to spare me the loathsome task of tithing the fishermen. I glance back at the unconscious mermaid. She'll need her strength if she is to heal. I crawl back under the shed with the day's catch and submerge the cage within the fish-woman's reach. Crab rots immediately upon dying, rendering it inedible. Submerged in the trap, it will survive long enough for the creature to feast on it for breakfast. Climbing back up into the shed, I wonder what mermaids eat in the wild. Fish, I suppose. What else would they consume?

***

The mermaid takes up all the conversation around the dinner table. Father listens dispassionately as my sister describes how swiftly it moved in the water and my pinheaded brother goes into an outlandish description of the mermaid's gigantic fangs and horns and claws. It had tentacles, he insists. And a snout like a swordfish. And it was naked and without clothes!

Father raises a hand to halt his running mouth. "Stop talking, Pitr."

"And wings!" Pip claims, snot running down his face. "It had angel wings!"

"Quiet!"

Silence follows the fist on the table. Even Pip has enough sense to lower his eyes and wipe his nose. Father's face hardens, the scowl biting deeper. The news of the mermaid distresses him. Why? Perhaps because there is no mention of such creatures in our sacred texts. There are giants and trolls in the Book of Sorrows & Indiscretions, and there are dragons and witches aplenty in the Proverbs of Carcosa, but no mermaids. There is Serpentus, the giant sea monster that ruled chaos until the One True God slew it, using its carcass to create the earth. Is the creature under the fishing hut related to it somehow?

Bryndis is the first to break the silence. "Where did it come from? Why is it here?"

These same questions keep circling the conversation, turning speculation wilder with each orbit. I imagine the same discussions are being debated at every supper table in the village. Riddles without solutions. The Reverend Uriah remains silent, not offering any speculation as to where the creature came from or what it wants.

Bryndis is still talking. "Did God create such a creature?" she asks. "Or did the Devil?"

Father broods. He sets the spoon down. Pip makes a face at our sister.

Bryn's conjectures set my own mind turning. Without

meaning to, I utter aloud my thoughts. "What if there are things older than God?"

The bowls jump when the fist comes down again. I've gone too far. My father's eyes are blacker than coal.

"Do you think you're being funny, Kaspar? Blasphemy amuses you, does it? Makes you sound clever?"

He dabs his beard and hurls the napkin to the table. Walks away. A door slams. The three of us sit there like turnips, scolded.

Pip rattles the spoon against his teeth. "Do you think she has a name?"

Bryndis is irritable. "Don't be silly. Do fish have names?"

"Everything has a name." Pip scratches his armpit, chasing a flea. He holds it up to the light. "Even this flea has a name."

"Is that so?" sneers Bryndis. "And what is that pest's name?"

"Flea."

Bryndis throws her hands up and we clear the table. As pumpkin-headed as he is, Pip can run circles around anyone in an argument.

*** 

I lied when I vowed to tell no one of the mermaid's existence. There is one person I am desperate to tell, but there is little of hope of doing so. I wake early the next day and stoke the fire in the kitchen. Hook the cauldron over it to make father's tea. He prefers coffee, but we haven't had any in over two years. The trading ships rarely stop in our remote port.

I run down to the pier to see if she's there, helping her husband with his nets, but Gunther is alone. He hails me, asks after my health. He's much friendlier since yesterday's adventure. I ask if the mermaid has been spotted, but Gunther says no.

"She's probably dead on the bottom of the sea," he says. "With my best harpoon stuck in her."

Wishing him well, I stride through town, taking a

meandering route past the smithy's forge and around the net weaver's stall. I slow my pace when I come to Gunther's cottage. It is a sad-looking hovel with a sagging roof and a door that tilts badly in its frame. Knocking on Agnet's door would not be wise. Her neighbors would see. Visiting a wife while the husband is fishing is simply not done in our village. Well, it is, but it is done on the sly, and by cleverer men than myself.

The street is empty, so I knock. There is no answer. Stepping back, I see no smoke from the chimney. She must be out, so I hurry home.

Passing the tanner's hut, I spot Titus flensing a dolphin carcass. I wave hello, but, as usual, he pretends not to see me. We used to be best friends, Titus and I. As boys, we speculated endlessly on the mysteries of the wedding night, often taking turns playing bride and groom to unlock the riddle of the conjugal bed. Until Father caught us. He caned us both that day. Since then, Titus refuses to speak to me, or even acknowledge me in public.

Father has a list of chores for me, all of which I ignore as I scurry down the passageway to the fishing shed. I have with me a salve that Bryndis made to treat injuries. It is a foul-smelling ointment of eel grease and lavender, but it helps to close open wounds. Will it work on scaly flesh?

The mermaid's eyes are open when I splash into the water under the shed. She neither startles nor recoils at my appearance. Was she expecting me? I am surprised to find the crab untouched in its trap. Does she not realize it's for her, or does she dislike the taste of crab? Not everyone cares for it.

I don't want to frighten her. I want to reassure the creature that I mean no harm.

"Are you feeling any better?"

Her eyes are green upon green. The mouth is a flat line, betraying nothing. If there are fangs, I do not see them.

I hold up the pot of ointment. "I brought something for the wound. Will you let me salve it?"

She makes no reaction, so I ease my way closer. I am distracted by the odd way she blinks until I see that she has two sets of eyelids. An outer one like mine, but there is an inner lid that is a clear membrane like that of a frog. These strange lids make a wet clicking sound when she blinks.

The wound in its ribs has stopped bleeding, but it is still raw looking. She lies half-submerged in the sea water, the tail below and the maiden part above the water line. I notice tiny minnows darting all around the tail, pecking at the scales. Are they cleaning her wounds or devouring her one tiny nibble at a time?

I scoop some of the ointment from the jar. "I am going to put this on your wound. Understand?"

The greasy salve barely sticks to the glistening skin. I apply gobs of the stuff, but I do not know if it will close the harpoon gash. When my clumsy hand grazes her prickly nipple, she bolts upright and pops her jaw. The sharp teeth clamp onto my wrist like a thousand bee stingers and I shriek, splashing away as fast as I can.

We stare at one another in silence. Did she mean to hurt me, or was it simply a natural instinct to protect herself? My wrist throbs, and my mind immediately alights on the possibility of venom. Lord knows, there are plenty of sea creatures that kill with their poison. Is she any different? The exertion seems to exhaust the creature, and she slips below the water. Her expression remains inscrutable, but for a moment, I think I see a flash of regret in those strange eyes.

"Here," I say, setting the pot on a dry rock. "Heal yourself."

Keeping a safe distance, I tug the rope and draw the trap to me. If she doesn't want the crab, then we will eat it for our supper tonight.

# 7

THE CRAB IS BOILED and brought to the table. Father is delighted and Bryndis tears into it like a pirate. Pip won't touch it at all. My wrist throbs where the thing's teeth sank into it, the flesh swelling and jaundiced. When my sister asks what happened, I mutter something about the crab pinching me when I pushed it into the bubbling cauldron.

The surprise delicacy brings a rare touch of good spirits to our table. It is nice to see Father enjoy himself. I take no joy in it, the meat chewy and tasteless on my tongue. I am preoccupied with the secret hidden beneath the fishing hut. What if the creature dies? I tell myself that I have done all I can for it, but my stomach curdles on this lie. Do I not have some obligation to save such a fantastic creature? What if she is the last of her kind? The sourness of my indecision poisons my appetite. I push the plate away.

"Something wrong with your dinner?"

"No, sir."

"Then, what is it?" Father asks. "You've nary said a word all day."

"I am not hungry."

"Come, come, Kaspar," he says, sucking meat from the shell. "Out with it. What's bothering you?"

I take the foreclaw from my plate and turn it, examining its pointed contours. "What does the mermaid mean?"

"Mean? It doesn't mean anything. It's a bedtime story for children. A scrap from some old legend."

I point the claw at him. "If the mermaid exists, then what does that say about the Almighty? Does he allow this creature to live or is it beyond—"

"Enough." He aims a greasy finger at me. "There'll be no more blaspheming in this house. And no more talk of this wretched mermaid. You were all deluded by a trick of the light. There is no mermaid. End of discussion."

My jaw aches from clamping my mouth shut, from holding it all inside. In the end, my tongue betrays me.

"It's real," I say. "It is hiding under our fishing hut as we speak."

Reverend Uriah blusters up another dismissal, but a second glance at my face blunts his conviction.

"Show me."

I lead the way through the crypt and down the stone passage to the fishing hut. All four of us dip into the knee-high water and peer at the scaly being huddled there. Father is trembling, his eyes bulging from his head. Bryndis lets out a gasp. Pip goes straight to it as if to embrace the creature. Father yanks him back to safety.

"Go and fetch Gunther," he says. "And the other fishermen. Tell them to bring their nets and harpoons. Quickly now."

"Father, no," I protest. "It's wounded."

He won't listen, pulling his children away from the thing coiled in darkness. "Go. Now!"

\*\*\*

I do as I am told. What choice do I have? The men, roused from their evening pipes, gather their hooks and nets. One man, Clovis, retrieves the family broadsword from its place on the mantel, and hurries to catch up. They follow quickstep down the corridor, marching over the flagstone like knights of old, eager to carve their names into a saga of their own making. Most gasp when they see the fish-woman, some invoke God's name. A few titter with some strange delight, as if they have been anticipating this moment their whole lives.

All look to Gunther the Brave for direction. He orchestrates the approach, directing the men with nets and those with spears. Father insists the men capture it without killing it. Gunther closes in on the prey, and the others follow. Clovis, who is a slight man, can barely hold aloft his family sword. When it falls from his thin hands and splashes into the water, Gunther gives the signal and the men pounce.

A bedlam of shouting and rollicking, but they have her. Trapped in the great nets, the men haul the creature up into the hut and drag her back up the passageway. She twists and hisses at her captors, too weak to slash through the netting. Step over stone step, they break out into song. Clovis is left behind, frantically searching the water for his family heirloom. The man is in tears, believing he has cursed his future generations.

He isn't alone. What have I done? Telling father was a mistake. Had I truly expected him to be sympathetic to the creature's plight? I have the head of a scarecrow, filled with nothing but moldy straw.

By the time the troop hauls their catch to the square, the whole village has come to see what all the singing is about. The fountain in the village square is not very big, but it is deep. They roll the creature into it and withdraw their nets. The fountain water is brackish and smells of sulfur. A line of villagers forms quickly from the square to the shore, buckets passing hand-to-hand to fill the cistern with seawater. The water level rises to a depth sufficient enough to allow the creature movement, but shallow enough to prevent her from climbing out. Every soul crowds around the stone lip to wonder and squeal in delight at the strange thing they have captured. The mermaid sinks to the bottom and gazes back at the leering faces above.

Debate erupts throughout the onlookers over what to do with the fabled thing. Some demand they set it free, claiming that keeping a mermaid captive will bring nothing but disaster. Others argue the opposite, insisting that the creature will bring good fortune to our destitute settlement. People will come from all over to gaze at our prize, they argue. The harbor will crowd with vessels from every kingdom and the curious will flood their streets, eager to pay for the once-in-a-lifetime chance to see an actual mermaid. Gunther is eager to fry it up to see what mermaid tastes like. A few of the fishermen lust after it, openly speculating how one would mount such a creature. It's all fish below the waist, says one. It's still just a woman, shrugs his companion.

Jugs of liquor are brought out and passed around. Someone saws at a fiddle and the night rolls on with merriment as people dance around the fountain. Gunther the Brave is exalted for his cunning, even though his part in the capture was no more than any man's. People love their heroes, I suppose. They try to lift Gunther onto their shoulders, but the harpoonsman is too heavy, and they all tumble to the cobblestones in a heap.

There are endless, drunken discussions on where the fish-woman has come from and why it is here. Did the storm wash it into the bay or had the full moon lured it to our shores? The pious denounce it as a devil, while the reprobates insist it is an angel sent from Paradise to save us.

Cornelius, the Prefect of our parish, pooh-poohs this as nonsense. "Everyone knows that mermaids are born without souls," he says. "This creature is here to steal a soul from one of our women. Best you girls stay away from it and keep your thoughts clean."

Hagar, the midwife, brazenly dismisses him as a fool. "Your ignorance is showing, Cornelius. Mermaids are the souls of murdered women, lost to the sea. Even a child knows that."

Sligo makes sport with this, joking that if this was true, the harbor would be overrun with mermaids. The fishermen slap one another on the back and laugh like apes.

Their wives do not laugh.

***

I wake the next morning with a dry mouth and stale vapors in my skull. My routine of starting the morning fire is abandoned as I venture out to the square to check on the mermaid. There are still a few scoundrels stumbling about and refusing to go home. A number of men lay snoring on the cobblestones. I step over them and look down into the fountain. The creature is there, swimming round and round the circumference of the cistern. The sight of it is troubling. I toss pebbles into the water to get her attention, but the mermaid does not look up or cease her endless laps.

More souls have slipped away from their beds this morning to come see the wondrous thing in the stone tank. Girls mostly, tiptoeing to the lip of the fountain. I need to get back, as I'm sure the household will be up. Father will be wondering why I am shirking my chores. A few more minutes, I bargain. It is difficult to tear away from the sight of the circling fish-woman.

"She's wonderful, don't you think?"

The voice slips in beside me, catapulting my heart into my throat.

Agnet smiles and dips the tiniest of curtsies to me. Her eyes are droopy with sleep, her hair haphazardly tucked into a coil. All of it is mine for a little while.

"You look tired," I answer. "Did you sleep poorly?"

"Hardly a wink. Gunther came home in a boisterous mood with a whole crew and insisted on regaling them with his tales."

"How crass," I say. She simply shrugs and gazes down at the water.

"They say you found her. Under the fishing hut?"

I tell her that this is true. "I'm such a fool. I never should have told Father about it."

Agnet stiffens at this. "All the men were there, in the hut?"

"Yes. Why?"

"Did anyone see it?"

"Of course, they saw it. She was right there under the floorboards."

"Not her," Agnet whispers, eyes darting around. "What you carved."

Our initials inside the heart. No wonder she looks so worried. I shudder to think what her husband would have done had he seen it. How stupid of me.

"No one saw it," I assure her.

Her shoulders relax. We watch the mermaid lap the pool.

"You should get rid of it, Kaspar. Scratch it out or rip the whole board up. He will kill me if he finds out."

The thought of destroying our mark will kill me, but I do not tell her this. Agnet has enough to worry about, and seeing how her hands wring, her fear is genuine. No one knows of our trysts in the fishing hut. Her husband would not react kindly were he to learn of it. Like all grooms, he assumed that his bride was as pure as the first snowfall.

"I'll scratch it out. Don't worry."

"I'm sorry."

There are more gawkers now, ringing the fountain to see the mermaid. All girls, oddly enough. They seem mesmerized.

"I saw a fox do this once," Agnet says.

"Do what?"

She nods at the sea-maiden going around and around. "My father trapped a fox and tried to tame it. The animal just circled the cage like this, going mad."

"Did he let it go?"

"No," she says, gathering her shawl about her. "The fox refused to eat or take water. It died after a few days."

# 8

THE WOOD IS THICK, but it is old and desiccated from the salt air. Prying the whole plank from the floor takes little effort. I trace a fingertip through the contours of her initials in the wood and conjure up the feel of her freckled skin. The divot in the small of her back and the sharpness of her hip bones, like the tips of icebergs under her flesh. How long has it been since I have kissed those sacred places?

Being with Agnet was a catastrophe of feelings, all overwhelming and confusing, but beautiful in a way that shocks me now. Bliss, longing, gratitude, heartache, and a hundred more feelings crashing one over the other like waves against the rocks. So much of it, and all at once, all crammed together in a heady stew. I became drunk on it. Where did it all go? All that is left now is this constant ache deep inside, and this dried out length of wood that bears our names. It's unfair that I have to destroy this keepsake. I lost her fossil and have no others; no lock of hair or even a love note to linger over.

I am an idiot, mourning over a block of wood. But it remains a dangerous thing for Agnet, so I pitch it as far as I can out to sea. It bobs, flashing on the waves, until the current carries it away and I cannot see it anymore. It is done. She is safe. Does anything else matter?

When I return to the church, my father's voice is echoing through the rafters, calling my sister's name. There is no reply, which only sharpens his tone.

"Where is your sister?"

"I don't know. The kitchen?"

His face is red from hollering. "I have looked everywhere. She is not here. Did she run off to see that pauper's son?"

My face remains stone. I play the fool. "Who?"

"Calder, that beggar boy." He wags a finger meant for my sister at me. "I've told her to stay away from that lad. She is betrothed to Sligo now."

I didn't know he was aware of Bryndis' sweetheart. How could he not, of course. Our sister has taken to weeping in the pantry over her upcoming nuptials.

"She said nothing to me about it," I tell him. "I'm sure she'll return soon."

He stops pacing, looks at me. "What is wrong with your hand?"

The swelling on my wrist has not abated. The mermaid bite is painful. I have taken to cradling my hand inside my shirt to protect it.

"It's nothing."

"Let me see."

He does not like the swelling nor the yellowy discolor of it. The ring of teeth marks are still visible and when he asks what made it, I tell him the truth.

"The thing has venom," he says, turning the wrist to the light of the window. "Does it sting?"

"Only if I bump it against something. Otherwise, it's numb."

"Did it speak to you? Down there, under the hut?"

"No, sir. I spoke to it, but I do not think we speak the same language."

He lets go of my arm. "Would you say it has some intelligence, this thing? Or is it just a wild animal? All instinct and appetite?"

I tell him it is highly intelligent. You can see it in her eyes. She is like us. My father's mouth twists, finding the idea distasteful.

"Father," I say respectfully, "do you think the mermaid has a soul? Like we do?"

"Do fish have souls? Do sharks pray?" He finds the idea amusing. "Only man has a soul, Kaspar. I should think you would know this. Have I failed my own son in his moral teachings?"

"No, sir."

A sneeze sounds from the doorway. Pip stands there watching us. He sports a blue cap on his bulbous head, and nothing else.

"Pitr," grumbles my father. "For goodness sakes, put some clothes on."

Pip removes the hat and wipes his nose with it.

I turn to my brother. "Pip, where is Bryndis?"

"She's with the others."

Father is already out of patience. "What others?"

"The other girls," Pip says. "Gone to see the luremaid."

\*\*\*

Pip is telling the truth. Our sister is at the fountain, watching the mermaid along with every other girl in town.

"What the devil is going on?" Father sputters when we reach the square. "Has every child abandoned their homes?"

"It would appear so," replies Lothar, the blacksmith. He too has come to find his errant daughters. "I woke to a cold hearth and no tea."

Father is livid. "What's gotten into them? Something is amiss here."

It is an odd sight, the village daughters ringing the pool like sentries, eyes fixed on the creature below.

Ulric, a fisherman whose beard is as long as his tales of fish that got away, is incensed at the sight of it. "They've all been bewitched, is what's wrong here. Abandoning their duties to come gawk at this monster. It's diabolical."

I pluck our sister from the throng, hoping to spare her father's punishment. It is not easy. I have to drag her away.

"Hurry home, Bryndis. Before father blows his top."

"I don't want to," she says, her eyes clinging to the pool.

"Father's temper is already on the boil. Do you want him to get his cane? Go."

She refuses to budge until Pip takes her hand and tugs her toward the church. I do not like the look in her eyes. Bryndis is not one to disobey or shirk her duties. I don't know what has possessed her like this.

The other girls are shooed away, their fathers and brothers shaming and scolding them for abandoning their tasks. The men remain, studying the creature that has caused all this commotion.

Sligo, the big-nosed widower, rests a boot on the lip of the fountain and spits into the water. "Maybe this is a mistake," he says, wagging his chin at the woman below. "She'll bring nothing but trouble, like any woman."

Lothar scratches at something in his armpit. "Do we kill it? Or just let it go?"

I cross to the stone lip and look down. The mermaid is no longer circling the perimeter. She lurks a few inches below the surface, looking up at the men. She does not look well. Paler than before, with scales molting from her tail. The smell rising from the water is sour.

"Reverend Uriah," says Sligo. "Are you all right?"

Father cranes forward, staring down into the water. "My eyes are troubling me. She looks just like Cordelia." He rubs his eyes and looks again. "See? She's the spitting image."

What is he talking about? The mermaid looks nothing like our mother. Granted, her memory has faded a little and sometimes I cannot recall her face very well. But the being below looks nothing like the Reverend's late wife. Is Father losing his eyesight? An unwise fate for a vicar.

Lothar scoffs at this. "What are you talking about, Reverend? The woman looks exactly like my Goneril, gone these six years."

Sligo, the oaf betrothed to my sister, dismisses both and declares that anyone with eyes can see that the mermaid bears an uncanny resemblance to his late wife. She was found face-down in this very fountain on the feast day of Saint Hathor. Gerda, as Sligo tells it, was fond of drink and merriment.

Are they all losing their eyesight, I wonder? Or their minds? Three widowers, all seeing the face of their dead wives in the countenance of the sea-woman. I tug at Father's sleeve, urging him to come home. As with Bryndis, I have to use a little force before he relents.

And yet, just as I drag Father away, the mermaid turns to me. The moment is brief. Her lips part in almost a smile and there, between the two front teeth, is a significant gap. The same shape and space as Agnet's. I shudder and tell Father to come away.

# 9

MY FATHER'S WORDS rankle me. Why had he thought that the woman in the pool resembled his dead wife? The mermaid looks nothing like Mama. And what of the other widowers; Lothar and Sligo? They too saw their lost brides reflected in the creature's face. The implications of it do not sit well. What was it the midwife had said? Mermaids are the lost spirits of murdered brides? Does that mean the good Reverend Uriah murdered our mother? I am aware of the nasty gossip about mother's fate, about how she had taken her own life because of her husband's cruel treatment. Is this true? Or is the worst possibility the actual truth? That he murdered her and threw her into the sea to cover up his awful crime? Does this also mean that the blacksmith and the long-nosed fisherman had murdered their wives, as well?

I cannot puzzle it out. Did I not also see Agnet's gap-toothed beauty reflected in the luremaid? Does this dispel my suspicion that Mother was murdered, or is it a portent of some tragedy yet to play out?

These terrible thoughts nibble at my brain the way the rat natters at a sack of winter grain. They distract me from my duties. I all but butcher the herring when I clean it and let a crockery plate slip from my clumsy hands to shatter on the floor. It had belonged to mother, an heirloom handed down through her family. Now it lies in pieces at my feet. Father scolds my clumsiness, asking if my brains have leaked out of my wide ears to render me a simpleton.

45

When the table is cleared, he asks me to brew the tea and orders Bryndis to prepare a plate of seedcakes. The village elders are meeting in the church at sundown. The matter of the mermaid is to be decided tonight.

My sister and I do as we're told, bringing the tea to the church. The blacksmith arrives with Ulric, the elder fisherman. Clovis, Bjarni, and Sligo follow, all stinking of fish and brine as they tuck into the tea and cakes. Prefect Cornelius apologizes for being late and Gunther the Brave arrives last. Unapologetic, he sprawls into a pew like he owns the place. Father dismisses us and then takes quorum. Bryndis and I have barely made the door when the men fall into a clamor over their predicament. Bryndis hisses at me to hurry, but I hold back, slipping into a shadow in the transept. I want to hear the council's decision.

My father is not one of the councilmen, but as parish minister, he is expected to mediate the discussion. Cornelius, as Prefect, holds authority in our little village, but the other men dislike him and openly flout his decrees. His gnarled cane acts as a gavel when he bangs it to restore dignity to the squabbling council.

The first order of business is the whereabouts of Hrolf, one of our more prosperous fishermen. He has apparently vanished from the village and his wife is beside herself with worry. According to Bjarni, no one has seen him since the night of revelry when they tossed the mermaid into the fountain.

"My memory of that night is a little foggy," admits Ulric.

"You were barking at the stars, if I remember correctly," Gunther laughs.

Ulric turns red. "Who saw Hrolf last?"

"I did," Clovis replies. "Later that night, when everyone had gone home. He was at the fountain."

"What was he doing?"

Clovis shrugs. "Pissing into it."

The councilmen grow quiet. No one says aloud what they all must be thinking.

Prefect Cornelius grows impatient, tapping his cane to hurry things along. "Hrolf will return on his own or wash up on the beach. Next order of business, please."

It is the mermaid in the cistern, and what to do with her. The councilmen break into arguments over her fate. Cornelius scolds them all for their chattering and says that if they cannot come to a decision, he will write to the palace court for direction in the matter. The men deride his ruling and resume their squabble.

"We shall wait for a response from the king," he says, striking his cane against the floor one last time. "The decision will be his."

He is jeered and scoffed at for his usual dithering. Gunther advocates for killing the creature, as it has become a nuisance. He offers to perform the duty himself. For a fee, of course. He will boil the bones down so they can be hung here in the church next to their relic of our sacred sea monster. Surely, the two are related, he says. The blacksmith is against this plan, advising that they keep the creature as a pet. Let people pay to see it, he says. The curious will fill our pockets with silver. Everyone wins.

Ulric, as the oldest fisherman in the village, and the most respected, declares that plan to be foolish. The mermaid is unnatural, an abhorrence to both God and man, and keeping it will only bring misfortune. He insists the creature be set free immediately. It is already wreaking havoc, he adds, noting how every maiden in the village is shirking her duty to come gaze at the mer-maiden. They practically worship it, he huffs.

The remaining councilmen, Bjarni, Clovis, and Sligo, are spineless reeds who sway with each argument, unable to make up their minds. The discussion grows animated, until my father steps in to put it to a vote. He lays out the choices and five of the seven hands rise in favor of allowing Gunther to gut the creature.

Tomorrow, the harpoonist will perform his duty and the

nuisance will be over. Prefect Cornelius is still prattling on about seeking counsel from the palace, but no one is listening.

The wise men of Torgrimsvær shake hands and leave.

***

I am sick to my stomach. The mermaid is sentenced to death and her blood will be on my hands. Why did I tell Father? Had I expected him to be merciful? I should have kept the secret to myself. I should have told only Agnet like I had planned. At least I know she can keep a secret. Now, it is too late.

The candle flickers from a draft in the wall. Both siblings are in bed when I return, and father withdraws into his room. I shake my sister awake and tell her of the council's decision. She sits up in alarm.

"We can't just let them kill it," I say.

"What are we to do about it? The men have made up their minds."

The tallow flutters again. Pip purrs loudly in his cot.

"We are going to set it free."

My sister won't hear of it. "You want to go against Father? And the council? They'd put us in irons."

"We have to, Bryndis. I am going to set it free, and you are going to help me."

"Don't be an idiot, Kaspar. Go to sleep."

She turns to the wall, and I hate my sister in this moment. I will need help if I am to get the creature out of the fountain and back to the sea. I look over at Pip. Our brother is simple-minded, but he is stronger than he looks. Loyal as a puppy, Pip will do anything I ask him to. I reach for his shoulder to wake him.

Bryndis shoots up, her face angry in the tallow light.

"Do not involve Pip in this," she hisses. "I will murder you if you get him in trouble."

She will, too. As the oldest, Bryndis feels responsible for us all, but she is overly protective of our little brother.

Chastened, I blow out the candle and wait until my father's snores deepen and everyone is asleep. Then I rise, carrying my shoes in hand until I am safely outside.

The moon is waning, but it offers enough light to see my way. I take the wheelbarrow from the yard and push it over the cobbles to the village square. I worry the racket will wake every household, but the eternal roar of the surf masks the clattering noise. This is my plan; get the mermaid in the barrow, wheel her down to the water, and tip her in. Exactly how I will get the creature out of the pool is another matter altogether. Leaning over the stone rim, I look for the mermaid, but the water is too dark to see anything. Has she escaped? That seems doubtful, considering how sickly she looked the last time I saw her. Perhaps someone else has rescued her? In my mind, I picture a scenario where all the village girls assemble to pull the creature from this filthy pool and wade her out into the waves. It seems almost holy, that image.

I am wrong in both assumptions. A form grows within the murky depths, floating to the scummy surface. Face down, back to the air, the way the dead float. Praying I am not too late, I grip the woman by the arm and haul and tug and strain until the great tail flops over the lip to dry land. Her eyes are open but milky. If the gills move, I cannot see it. I haul her into the wheelbarrow and fold the enormous tail around her. Scales flake away under my hands, slicing into my palms.

The route to the stony beach will be easier than the pier. All downhill, but the wooden wheel grinds against the pebbles and will go no further. Hooking my arms around her, I drag the mermaid into the foamy brine and let her go.

The waves rock her gently, her eyes up at the sliver of moon, and then she rolls over, face down in the water. The sailfin on her dorsal lies limp. She is dead. My foolish rescue has come too late. I wade back onto the shore and sit on the pebbles. I don't know why I want to cry. It is just a fish.

My thoughts turn to Agnet. They always do, but there is

a clarity here that startles me. I think back to the gap I had seen in the mermaid's teeth. How, in that brief moment, the mermaid had so eerily resembled Agnet that it had left me shaken. I remember now all the countless rescue plans I had made in the past. All daydreams and empty wishes.

My father had been the one to break the news of Agnet's nuptials to Gunther the Brave. Father knew I was fond of Agnet, although he did not know the extent of our secret liaisons. To his credit, he tried to be as gentle as he could with the bad news. I did not cry in front of him. I waited until I got to the fishing hut before letting it all blubber out.

Every night after that, I would dream up plans to rescue Agnet from her brutish husband. I would steal her away in the night and we would sail off in his boat. Or I would murder him in his sleep and take Agnet away. I would get him drunk and push him overboard. Poison his soup. Cast a spell so that a whale would swallow him whole. None of these fantasies involved besting Gunther in a fight. The man was a giant. He would have snapped me like a clamshell.

Of course, all these scenarios remained fantasies. I am no hero from a saga, rescuing a princess. I can do nothing, and Agnet is doomed to live out her days as a fisherman's wife.

So.

Maybe this is why I have foolishly attempted to save the mermaid. Agnet is lost, but maybe I could rescue this princess with the seaweed locks? Yet even this I cannot do as the creature is dead and I have failed. Her body sways in the shallows as the waves roll in and drain out again.

The tears come fast and easy now, me blubbering until my nose runs as bad as Pip's. When I finally dry my eyes, the carcass on the beach is gone.

# 10

PIP IS AGITATED the next morning, clattering his bowl of gruel without tasting a drop and prattling on about a bad dream he'd had. I stoke the morning fire back to life and tell him to pipe down. I am in no mood for his nonsense. I can't stop seeing the image of the mermaid rolling lifelessly in the surf. Bryndis indulges Pip, as she often does, by asking about his dream.

"Black clouds rolled in over the village," he says through the slime running down his face. "They blocked out the sun and did not go away. Every garden died. Then every hen, every goat. All the fish washed up dead on shore. The village died."

"It was just a dream," I tell him. "It doesn't mean anything."

Bryndis pats our brother's head and tells him not to think about it. "Eat your gruel."

The boy won't listen. "Something bad is going to happen. You'll see."

The discussion ends when father enters. Father hates talk of dreams. Not on any religious grounds, he just finds them excruciatingly boring. Even Pip knows enough to shut his flapping trap.

Father has barely tasted his breakfast when a hammering on the rectory door makes us all jump. Jon's son, Jasper, stands panting in our doorway, saying the Reverend is needed in the square. Something has happened. Father snatches his coat from the hook, orders us to stay put, and follows Jasper. Without a thought, Pip races out the door after him, and Bryndis follows. I know what the fuss is about, but I go after them, anyway.

The councilmen are present, along with half the village. The mermaid is gone, and everyone is upset. The men are angry, eager to know what has happened, especially Gunther, who has spent the morning sharpening his blade in anticipation of the slaughter. All the young daughters and sisters are sad, some openly sobbing as they look down into the now-empty fountain. The water smells worse than ever, emitting a noxious miasma that has everyone covering their nose.

Disagreements fling back and forth about what happened to their prize. Did the mermaid escape on its own, slithering over the wet cobbles to reach the sea? Did someone help it escape? Or has some greedy villain stolen it for his own twisted pleasure? Clovis, who is drunk, yammers on about how he had witnessed the mermaid burst into righteous flame and fly up to the heavens where it became a holy comet in the night sky. An act of divine retribution by the One True God. He is clouted about the head and driven from the square. Some are glad to see the end of it, declaring the whole thing a nuisance. Midwife Hagar says it is all for the best, as mistreating a mermaid will only bring bad luck.

I pull father aside. "Ask if they've checked the shoreline. Maybe its carcass washed up there."

Boys are dispatched to the beach and the jetty of craggy rocks that acts as a breakwater to the sea. They return breathless, with nothing to report. The hubbub grows stale, and villagers drift off to get on with their day. Wives shepherd their children home while the fishermen ready their boats for the day's haul. Our little saga is over, and everything can go back to normal now.

Walking back to the church, Bryndis lags beside me and keeps her voice down.

"Was it you?" she wants to know. "Did you set it free?"

"What does it matter? It's gone."

Her fingernails dig into my elbow so hard it hurts. My sister is unnaturally strong. "Did you do it? Tell me."

I kick a pebble. "I was too late. It was dead."

"Dead? What did you do with it?"

"Gave it back to the sea."

We walk on. "Probably for the best," she remarks. "I will miss it, though."

I agree. "We can all go back to our daily drudgery now."

Bryndis says nothing in reply, but her face sours at the thought.

***

My prediction proves true as the day rolls out without incident or deviation from routine. People avoid the village square because of the smell. A green scum has formed on the surface of the stagnant pool, trapping insects and a few small birds. Prefect Cornelius complains that it needs to be bailed and scrubbed, but when he asks for volunteers, everyone becomes busy with their chores.

It isn't until the fishermen return at the end of the day that any hint of trouble bubbles up to disturb the quiet of a dull afternoon.

Ulric complains that his nets have been torn up. He holds them up for us to see the gaping hole in the webbing. Sligo, tying his boat off, says the same has happened to him. His skiff is empty of catch. Bjarni, drenched to the bone, returns home in Brom's boat. Something had rammed his dory, causing it to capsize. He knows not if it was a whale or one of the blind sharks that prowl these waters. Brom, bobbing nearby, had witnessed the whole event and had rowed hard to pull his friend from the sea.

Even Gunther has suffered the same misfortune with a slashed net. Wall-eyed Wilfred shows us the splintered remains of his traps, all seven destroyed by something spiteful in the depths. The crowd on the wharf titters and speculates over what could have happened. Has the luremaid incited the fish to turn on the fishermen? It seems absurd.

I spot Agnet among the faces, rushing along the pier to see if her husband is injured. Her concern for him angers me. I am petty.

Adja Blundsquill is running to and fro along the stone dock, unable to find her husband's skiff among the others. He had gone out with the rest this morning but has not returned. A chill of concern ripples through the townsfolk. The sun is going down and a lone fisherman out on a dark sea is unlikely to return. Gunther untethers his boat and rows out to find him. Adja is circled by the other women who assure her that her husband will return.

Down on the beach, I see young Tito calling for his dog, and asking if anyone has seen him. No one has. Why this troubles me, I cannot say.

The day becomes peculiarly still. The sea settles into glass when the breeze drops. Fishermen look up as their vessels cease bobbing, and the cries of the gulls echo clear across the bay. With no wind, the smell of dead jellyfish on the beach rises to my nose, unpleasant but familiar. The village tucked behind the wharf, with its drab huts and clay-tiled roofs, is a picture waiting to be painted.

And still, Tito calls for his missing pet.

Someone on the far end of the wharf is hollering his fool head off, pointing to something out in the bay. A lone figure cuts silently over the surface of the water. The sail of the dorsal fin arcs high above the surf. The mermaid observes us for a moment before slipping beneath the waves.

She has survived! A sense of relief washes over me like an ablution. The sea creature is alive and free to return to whatever magical kingdom it came from. Away from this awful place that sought to slaughter it. Some grouse at this, but a surprising number of the villagers share my sentiment. A few even clap their hands as if to congratulate the maiden in the water. Ulric shakes a bony fist at it, while Mesud raises his harpoon, hoping it will swim within range.

She is spotted again, on the east side of the quay this time.

But much closer. Again, she slices the surface at a brisk clip, her strange eyes on us. As before, the same questions come as we stare back at it. What does it want? Why doesn't it just swim away?

Standing close to Hagar, I hear the midwife mutter to the other women. "She came with the full moon," she whispers. "She can't leave until the next one."

How Hagar comes by this knowledge, I cannot say, but I suspect there is more to the woman than just midwifing babes into the world.

Gunther rows back in and tells Adja that he is sorry, but he could not spy her husband's skiff anywhere. His face darkens when the others tell him of the mermaid's return. There is a splash on his starboard side. When the creature breaks the surface a third time, Gunther watches her glide past with a calculating gaze. Tugging at his trousers, he draws out his pizzle and pisses into the sea.

***

I am not witness to how the calamity unfolds the following day. I see only its aftermath. It occurs in the early morning, while I am stirring the scullery coals to life. By the time I run down to the pier, all I see is the blood and the panic on everyone's faces. After speaking to those who had witnessed the incident, I can stitch together something close to a narrative of the bloodbath.

The fishermen had returned to their skiffs and sloops in the morning light. They had mended their nets and repaired their wooden traps, each man eager to make up for yesterday's lack of catch. Eight boats left the pier that morning. Only five would return. A few of the fishermen were wary of venturing out since the mermaid had been spotted again. A mermaid would scare all the fish away, they said. These men changed their tunes when they saw Gunther the Brave climb into his sloop with sharpened harpoons, coils of new rope, and two oarsmen to propel his craft. He told the men that he was not fishing today. Nay, this morning, he was hunting mermaid. Emboldened, the reluctant fishermen cast off and rowed out into the bay after him.

Hugo's boat was the first to be struck. He had let the oars rest to light his pipe when his vessel was hit from below, throwing him to the keel. His pipe was knocked overboard. Looking at the bow, he saw seawater spewing in from a break in the hull. He was sinking.

One of the fishermen—it is unclear who—hollered at his fellows, pointing to something in the water. "Look! Yonder, she breaks!"

The fishermen on the bay and the people on the pier all saw the creature break the surface, its long, eel-like tail arcing up out of the waves.

Gunther was already on its scent, roaring at his crew to row as he readied a harpoon. When the sail of the mermaid sprang from the sea, he hurled his spear with the ferocity of Torgrim wielding his flaming sword. He missed. Cursing in the language of all sailors, he scrambled to reel the weapon back for another strike.

Bjarni's skiff was struck next, rammed with such force that it capsized. Thrown overboard, the red-haired fisherman flailed about in the chop, calling for help.

Gunther's voice was heard echoing over the bay. "Come about, lads! Starboard now. Row, you cockless bastards!"

Sligo sang out when he saw the mermaid breaking again. With her fin slicing the water, her trajectory compassed straight to the floundering man. Those on shore heard his screams, but the fishermen saw the carnage with their own eyes. Bjarni was shaken to and fro in the manner of a shark attack and the water frothed with his blood. Brom said the man was dead before the monster pulled him under.

Gunther, although not in position, launched another spear. Ulric, who was nearby, leaned over the gunwale and slashed the water with a cutlass. Sligo had a rope ready to fling to the man in the water, but Bjarni did not surface.

The water was still for a moment. Gulls circled overhead, hungry for scraps.

"Sound off when you spot the bitch!" Gunther bellowed.

Every man scanned the water, but none saw her coming. Jon was standing in his skiff, harpoon held high, when the water spumed like a whale breaking. The mermaid shot from the sea and dragged the fisherman into the depths. When he bobbed to the surface a moment later, old Ulric was closest. He scrambled to pull Jon into his boat, but there wasn't much to save. The poor man had been savaged so viciously that there was nothing below his ribs.

Chaos churned the bay after that. Men screamed and beat the water with their oars, all sounding out at the sight of the creature. Arwyn's boat was rammed, the hull splintered. Mesud's skiff was capsized, its skipper screaming as he went into the sea.

Gunther fired all three of his harpoons each time the mermaid broke the surface. Old Ulric slashed the water with his sword. The other fishermen came about to rescue their fallen comrades. Arwyn and Mesud were pulled from the water, bloodied and screaming in terror.

All rowed like mad for the pier, save Gunther. His oarsmen, Osk and Brom, insisted they cut for land, but Gunther refused. Reeling his weapons back, he readied another strike. The mermaid slipped to the surface on his lee side, as if daring the whaler to try again. Osk swears she was smiling at old Gunther like this was all a game, but Osk was rambling when he told me his story. I cannot tell which details are true and which are imagined. Osk claims that the she-creature snatched Gunther's harpoon from the air and snapped it in two. Witnessing that, he and Brom rowed like mad for home, no matter how Gunther screamed at them for their mutiny.

This is the scenario I find when I arrive at the wharf. Five boats make it back to the pier, three lost at sea. Men scramble and jostle to back away from the water. The injured fishermen are lifted from the boats and the pier runs red with their blood. Arwyn has lost both legs, Mesud an arm. Their faces are white and their bodies jerk in spasms from the shock. They are ferried further ashore, everyone hollering for the midwife.

The mermaid cuts through the water close to the wharf, breaking surface to eyeball those of us on dry land. Ulric swears she is daring us to try again.

"Look," he snarls. "The bitch is gloating over her handiwork."

The bodies of Bjarni and Jon bob in the bay, torn like rag dolls. When one drifts close to the dock, Osk tries to snag it with a boathook, but the sea creature bursts from the depths to snatch the hook from his hands. Everyone runs and no further attempts are made to retrieve the dead men. They are still out there, rolling with the surf, as we all cower on the shore. The gulls circle and cry over the water. One alights on a bobbing corpse and pecks at the torn flesh.

Reeling his weapons back, he readied another strike.
The mermaid slipped to the surface on his lee side,
as if daring the whaler to try again.

# 11

ARWYN DOES NOT live to see the morning. With both legs chewed off, he has simply lost too much blood. Mesud clings to life, but he is senseless with a wide-eyed fever. Two attempts are made to fetch the remains of Bjarni and Jon from the water, both foiled by another mermaid attack. Clovis loses his skiff in the attempt but manages to swim to safety before the creature can eat him. Neither corpse is recovered. They are picked apart by the fishes and the birds, until there is nothing left to float.

The Prefect asks Father to arrange the burials, even though the coffins will be empty.

Some try to fish from the dock, casting their nets in, only to have them ripped from their hands. Gunther stalks the pier relentlessly with a harpoon in hand, eager for any chance to spear the monster. With each throw he takes, the mermaid rises to the surface to taunt him further. Most of us simply watch from the safety of the shore as she glides back and forth, patrolling the harbor. Anyone foolish enough to climb into their skiff quickly scrambles out again when the mermaid rushes for them. I have never seen anything move that fast.

This goes on for days. With the men unable to fish, larders and pantries soon empty out. There are only a few families that own cows, but these animals have all become sick. Blood squirts into the pail now, instead of milk. Eggs collected from every coop are spoiled, cracking out a gray sludge. Hagar's goat is found floating in the bay, and dogs begin to disappear.

In a place where fishing is everything, the village is going hungry. And the vicar's family, who depends solely on the kindness of its parishioners, goes hungry sooner than most. How can they contribute to the tithe, the fishermen ask, when their own barrels are down to last winter's dried fish heads?

The village council meets in the church again. We have nothing to offer but water. The men rail and curse at their predicament. Does the mermaid mean to starve them out by preventing them from doing the only thing they know how? If they cannot harvest the cod and the redfish now, they will certainly not last the winter. Are they being punished? Have they offended our One True God in some way? Is there some way to make contrition and make the monster go away? The good Reverend Uriah has no answer for them. All we can do, he tells them, is pray.

Gunther declares them all cowards and walks out in disgust. The rest drift off in ones and twos. Bryndis and I stand at the window, watching them leave. Pip hides under the table, complaining that he is hungry. Bryndis gives him a piece of dried eel skin to chew on.

***

Early morning, and the wharf is empty save for a lone figure framed against a pink sunrise. The fishermen and their wives stay away from the water now. There is just this solitary villager, staring out at the sea. The skies are cloudless and the water calm. There is the sound of gulls and the lapping of waves against stone. Of the sea creature, there is no sign.

I stride out to the pier, one eye on the water for any telltale ripple. "Agnet? It is not safe out here."

She turns slightly in acknowledgment but does not take her eyes from the sea. Her shawl is draped over her head like a veil and the sea spray is dampening the hem of her skirt.

"Come away from the water. Please."

"Nothing will happen, Kaspar," she says.

I take in the flat line of the horizon. "Tell me what you see out there."

"Escape?" she says. "If I row out in my husband's sloop and raise the sail, do you think the mermaid would try to sink me?"

"I think she would eat you like she did the others."

With the shawl hiding her face, all I see is one brown eye. "I don't think she would. I think she would let me sail away in peace."

Her thoughts tack to strange winds. "What makes you think she'd spare you?"

"Maybe she doesn't like the taste of women. Males seem to be her preferred delicacy."

"And goats, if you listen to Hagar. That poor woman is inconsolable over her pet."

"My mother once told me that the goat is her husband. When he tried to dither the skirts of the girl next door, Hagar brewed him a tea that transformed him into a goat."

I laugh. "I never met the fellow. Hagar's husband was gone before we settled here."

She still hasn't taken her eyes from the open sea. This troubles me.

"How long ago was that, Kaspar?" she asks. "How long have we known each other?"

"Five winters, I think." Five years, seven months. I look across to the pebbly beach. "You showed me how to hunt for fossils. Do you remember? You showed me the creatures trapped in the stone."

The memory of it is sweet; following Agnet along the beach while she turned over rocks, hunting for the magic ones that held a phantom trapped in stone. I remember how my nerves would crackle around her, as if every sense was tuned only to her voice, her smell, her laugh. It was an awkward, yet sweetly agonizing moment in time. Before our first kiss, but after I knew my heart was snagged on her hooks.

"I miss those days," I say.

She doesn't reply. I have heard people gossip about

Agnet. She has been married for a year now and still is not with child. The women whisper that she is barren, the men that she is unwilling. I wonder if it's through sheer force of will that she does not bear his child. I go so far as to wonder if Agnet refuses to consummate the marriage. That is a foolish thought, but I still think it.

The shawl drapes open to reveal a few more freckles on her face. Her eyes go to my hand tucked inside my shirt.

"Are you hurt?"

"The bite. It stings a little."

She insists on seeing it so I withdraw the hand from the folds of my shirt. The flesh is purple, the skin cracked like dried mud. Agnet is repulsed by it.

"Are you poisoned?"

"No," I reply too quickly. "It is nothing."

"Have you seen Hagar about it?" When I tell her I have not, she shakes her head. "Go see the midwife, Kaspar. Before that gets worse."

It's only when she turns to leave that I see what she is hiding. Her bottom lip is swollen and discolored.

My heartbeat ruptures my eardrums. I stop her. "Agnet, my God. Did he do this?"

"It's nothing."

"I'll kill him. I will murder him—"

She twists her arm out of my grip. "Stop it. The man would eat you alive."

"What happened? Why did he hit you?"

A sigh. Agnet looks up at the sky. No clouds. "He didn't mean it. He's not himself if he can't go out to sea. The poor man feels helpless and useless. His temper..."

I can't believe my ears. How can she pity the brute? After what he's done?

"Poor man?" I spit. "You care for him?"

She looks at me like I am a simpleton. "He's my husband. I have to."

"Do you have to make excuses for him, also?"

"Do not judge me," she says, curling her bruised lip into a sneer. "Ever. You have no idea."

"Agnet, I don't want to see you hurt."

"Don't presume to know me, Kaspar." She walks away, her brogans ringing sharply off the stone. "We're not children anymore."

***

The men of Torgrimsvær become useless. Unable to fish, unable to provide, they loiter in doorways and doze under their empty stalls. They spend their days in the grog hall or guzzle from jars of homemade brews. Poisonous potato brandy or cognacs so potent they cause blindness. They carouse over the cobbles and fight in the streets. Grown men, stripped to the waist, fists up and squaring off. Those that do not fight wager on those that do. Coins trade hands, debts are forgiven one moment only to be doubled the next.

A brave few try to hunt in the woods of the mountains only to return empty-handed, for there is nothing worth hunting there. Some return sickly and green from having munched on the eldritch mushrooms and woodland toadstools. Nero the Eel Skinner trips over an exposed tree root and spears his groin with his own lance. Hrodbert, who was always a poor shot with his bow, fires an arrow into his cousin's thigh.

Red-eyed and brazen with drink, the men sing sailor's rhymes to the women in the streets. Wives and daughters hurry past with reddened faces or gritted teeth. The fishermen hallo and cajole my father to beg God to smite the sea witch dead. Torgu Blackteeth has the mad idea of burning the mermaid by pouring a barrel of pitch into the harbor and setting it on fire. Some try to talk him out of it, but he scolds their cowardice and drunkenly rolls the barrel out to the pier. His headless body is found the next morning, washed up like driftwood on the stony beach.

As the food dwindles and the barrels are scraped, the men grow worse. Frustrated and red-eyed, they direct their rage at their wives, their children. The fisher-women move about the streets with blackened eyes and bruised cheekbones. When they speak, they cover their mouths to hide missing teeth. The children become street urchins, avoiding home out of fear of provoking their father's tempers.

I try not to think of what Agnet is enduring, but my traitorous thoughts always circle back to her. Lying on my cot at night, I devise elaborate schemes and trickeries to murder Gunther the Brave. I could pierce his heart with his own harpoon or strangle him with a guy rope. I could bludgeon his brains with an anchor or simply push his drunken hide into the sea and ring the dinner bell for the mermaid.

But I am a coward and, worse, a breaker of vows. I make no move to murder the brute and save Agnet. When I stand before the gates of paradise, the Almighty will cast my ragged soul into the pit for this, and this sin alone.

In place of action and resolve, I simply cry into my pillow until Bryndis scolds me to dry up and go to sleep. Pip, across the darkened room, sings another sea shanty.

# 12

THE THROBBING IN my wrist wakes me through the night. At dawn I am up and stirring the fire to life in the hearth. Our larder remains empty no matter how many times I check it. My palsied hand has swollen further and begun to smell. When my siblings come downstairs, I tell them I am going out. Pip wants to come along, but I tell him to stay here. The little twerp holds his breath.

"Take him with you," Bryndis sighs. "I'm in no mood for one of his fits."

We head north to the edge of Torgrimsvær where the hovels of town give way to the forest and the mountain range beyond. Here on the rutted path lies one last cottage hidden amongst the trees. A wisp of smoke rises from the chimney.

"Where are we going?"

I nod at the drab hovel ahead. "To see Hagar."

Pip stops. "The witch's cottage?"

"She's not a witch. Are you coming or no?"

He follows me, catching up to take my hand like he used to do when he was little. There is a moment after I knock on the oaken door before Hagar ushers us inside. She seems neither surprised nor unhappy to see us.

The cottage is dark and smells of woodsmoke and spices. Strange herbs and flowers dangle overhead, hung from the rafters to dry. Hagar is also the village culpepper. The floor is packed earth and there are seven cats watching my brother and I with suspicion. Before the hearth is a single rocking chair and a rough bench. The midwife motions for us to sit.

"Are you here about him?" she asks, nodding at my brother.

"No. He's beyond help." I slip my hand from the fold of my shirt. "It's this that needs mending."

Her gentle face pinches at the sight of it. It is ghastly. The flesh purpled, turning to black at the fingertips. Hagar leans in close, spies the ring of puncture marks.

"Something bit you?"

When I tell her what made it, there is a sharp intake of breath.

"I've never seen a mermaid bite before, let alone cured one. Is it painful?"

"It is mostly numb."

She studies it closely, turning it to the light and asking me to wiggle my fingers. She raises my hand to her nose and smells it.

"That stinks of rot, Kaspar. And that is not a good sign. The thing's venom is killing it."

Hagar does not mince words. She is not rude, but she does not lie or sugarcoat.

"Is there anything you can do for it?" I try not to sound like I'm begging.

She rises and runs a hand along the clay pots on the windowsill. She chooses one and returns to her rocking chair.

"We can try this, but I do not know if it will remedy it. The thing's venom is on your blood, and it is killing your hand."

"And if this doesn't work?"

"The rot will set in. The hand will have to come off before the venom creeps any further."

It is Pip who makes a noise this time. He is usually lost in his own head, but not now. He looks terrified at the midwife's proposed remedy. I shouldn't have brought him here.

Hagar gets a piece of hardtack from the table and gives it to my brother. "Take this," she says. "Wait outside."

He does as he is told, gnawing on the biscuit. Hagar looks at me.

"When did she bite you? How many days?"

I've lost track of the days and my brain is too fuzzy for counting. "A fortnight? Why?"

Hagar frowns. "I know nothing of mermaid bites. Who does, really? But I would think that mermaid venom would act quickly. A day. Two at the most. It's strange."

"What do you think it means?"

She inspects the wound again, the ring of teeth marks. "She's marked you for some reason. Perhaps she has something special in mind."

I ask what this might be, but she refuses to speculate. Putting the pot of ointment in my hand, she tells me to run along and bother her no more.

***

Our woodshed is down to its last few splinters of pine. I will need to bring Pip with me to the forest to scrounge up more firewood. It is difficult enough to split logs with a dull axe but doing so one-handed is beyond frustrating. My cursing is interrupted when our neighbor, Magda Bergden, appears at the gate. She asks if I have seen her daughter, Heloise.

"I haven't seen anyone, ma'am," I say, standing another block on the stump.

The woman frowns. "She should have started the mending by now. Is she in the church?"

I check the church, only to find it empty, and return to the irritated mother. "Has she gone to the water? Or to the meadow, to pick berries?"

"She'll get a good thumping if she has," Magda replies. "The girl is not herself these days."

Opening the rectory door, I holler out for my sister, thinking Bryndis might know, but there is no reply. When I holler again, Pip appears. He doesn't know where our sister is. I ask if he has seen Heloise from next door, but the little turnip claims he doesn't know anyone by that name.

And now, old Ulric has joined Magda in our yard. He too is missing a daughter and, like Magda, is extremely put out

68

by the inconvenience. The mystery is solved when Hagar, passing by with an armload of mustard stalks, overhears us.

"They've all gone down to the water," Hagar says, chucking a thumb in the direction of the sea. "Have you not seen them? The whole lot of them."

Magda, Ulric, and myself look out over the rooftops and down to the shoreline. Hagar speaks the truth. The pier is crowded by what appears to be every girl in the village, their backs to us, looking out at the sea.

I bark at Pip not to touch the ax, which he is trying to extract from the stump, and then I follow my companions down to the water. Old Ulric has taken to carrying his ancient cutlass with him wherever he goes. Tucked under his belt with his hand resting on the pommel, he says aloud what we are all thinking.

"What new trouble is this?" he grumbles. "Have we not had our fill of mischief?"

"Look at them all," huffs Magda, gathering her skirts as she marches. "Every lass in town, idling the day away when there's work that needs doing."

Ulric makes a laughable display of half drawing the cutlass. "A damn mutiny is what it is."

The sun is strong and the water in the bay ripples gently. Overhead, the terns call to one another.

Magda and Ulric both spot their errant daughters among the idle girls lining the pier. Bryndis is here, too, as is Agnet. None respond when called, their attention fixed on something out in the bay.

The mermaid is there, slipping through the surface of the water so gently that she leaves no wake. She moves gracefully, almost luridly, like a bather out for a midday dip. The girls on the pier are mesmerized with the same glassy look in their eyes as when they formed a ring around the fountain.

"Shameful," spits Ulric.

"Outrageous," agrees Magda.

More fathers and mothers are here, pulling and tugging their daughters away. They scold the girls for shirking their duties, they shame them for their idleness. They smack cheeks and twist their hair for being so weak-willed, for letting themselves become bewitched by the creature in the water.

"Tainted by the devil's mistress," grumbles the blacksmith.

"A good lashing will remedy this," hisses a fishmonger's wife.

I take my sister by the arm. "Come away, Bryndis. It's not safe." But she will not budge.

Then something happens, something that I have never witnessed before. The girls revolt. They slip free of their parent's grip to go back to the water's edge. Some even violently shove their fathers and mothers away. A bright and wild look flashes hot in their collective eyes. It is frightening.

Out on the water, the mermaid watches. Her webbed hand lifts from the ripples and beckons to the girls, urging them to join her.

First to last, the daughters of Torgrimsvær jump into the sea.

Terror and panic strike every heart. Girls flail and splash as their elders scramble to pull them out before they are slaughtered by the sea monster. I snatch my sister by the collar and heave up. When I look back to track the mermaid's position, she has gone under. The screaming and the horror doubles. I rush to save Agnet, but her husband beats me to it, plucking his bride from the churning waters with one hand. Dripping and choking, the girls are hauled onto the pier. Shoes are lost and hats blown off as all run for dry land. I push Bryndis along, terrified that the sea creature is nipping at our heels.

No one looks back until all collapse on the turf. Our panic was for naught as the mermaid hasn't rushed the pier at all. She bobs on the waves, watching us. Then she dips, her great tail breaking the surface, and she is gone.

Everyone trudges home. I watch Agnet being led away by her impatient husband, but her presence on the pier is something of a mystery. Why was she among the throng of unwed daughters and bereft widows? How unhappy is she? Are my suspicions correct in that Agnet does not return the love of her harpooner husband? Do I dare hope this to be true?

Hope. Such an ugly word, like a sore that will not heal.

# 13

LOCK UP YOUR DAUGHTERS, someone cries. Keep them safe from the sea hag, bellows another. Every girl is marched home and kept inside. Unmarried women are warned to stay indoors, widows are chased from the streets. Fuming over the incident on the pier, the fishermen storm the church, demanding my father do something. The pews fill up and people jostle for elbow room inside the church like it is the feast day of Saint Barquentine the Disconsolate. The pleasant aroma of polished wood and candle wax is overwhelmed by the reek of sour sweat and stale garments.

Taken aback by the siege of his own parishioners, Father urges the villagers to remain calm and explain what has happened. Bryndis, Pip, and I sneak to the door of the vestry to see what will unfold. The good Reverend Uriah turns pale when he learns how the mermaid bewitched their own daughters to jump into the sea. No one is safe, yammers Ulric. The sea creature is determined to murder us all, rails Magda from next door.

Father beseeches the raging parishioners to remain calm. "We must be resolute and faithful in this hour of trial," he says in an unsteady voice. "The All-Powerful will protect us."

"How?" demands Preben Drachmar, the boil lancer. "How will he protect us when the witch turns our own children against us?"

Brom raises his fist at the parson. "Day and night we pray, and still that beast is out there. God is deaf to our prayers!"

"He has turned his back on us," says a weepy voice from the back of the nave.

Father aims a finger at the unseen dissenter. "Do not do that, brother! Do not abandon Him when we need Him most."

Our father's voice is drowned out by the naysayers. Their fear boils over and distills into anger with raised fists and stomping feet. A glimmer of panic runs quicksilver over father's face, fearing the mob will rush the pulpit to tar and feather him. My siblings sense it, too. Bryndis claps a hand over her mouth. Pip bolts through the parishioners to cling to father's legs like a barnacle. To protect him, to shield him.

The clamor falters and dies. The collective rage cools at the sight of a terrified child rushing to his father's defense. The parishioners mumble and grumble. Pip turns to them, a thick membrane of mucous jiggling from his nose to father's trouser leg.

Lothar Palson stands up from his pew. "Someone among us betrayed our parish. Everything was fine when the creature was confined to the fountain." He pivots on his heel, rolling a suspicious eye over the throng. "Someone set the mermaid free."

Boots stomp the floor and heads nod in agreement with Lothar's deduction. Their voices rise and collide in the echoing vault of the church. Who has betrayed us? And why? Which among us was the bastard who freed the monster from the stone fountain? Neighbor glances uneasily at neighbor. No one is above suspicion and the tension blooms until it stifles every sound inside the church.

"Who?" they chant.

"Why?" they demand.

A clenched stillness suffocates every soul. Every ear cranes to hear a reply, to hear a shoe drop. Nothing.

It is Pip, of all people, to break the silence. Phlegm oozes down his pinched face as his hand lifts, the accusatory finger drawing aim on me.

"Kaspar did it," he stammers. "It was Kaspar who set the mermaid free. He didn't want her to die."

The blood runs out of my limbs as every head turns on me. My hands are numb, my feet useless stumps in my broken shoes.

The roar erupts all the way to the vaulted ceiling. A hand snatches my collar at the same moment a fist smites my ear. I am thrown to the floor. I see a flash of terror on my sister's face before the mob closes in to blot out the world.

***

Bryndis tells me later that father was helpless to stop them. He was shoved aside and cursed as a traitor while the mob dragged me down to the pier. Carried along by the throng, I lift my head to see the stone pier and the sea beyond that. A single figure waits at the end of the jetty, framed black against the honey-colored sunset. For one foggy moment, I think it is Agnet come to save me, but I am wrong. Her husband snatches me up by the collar with so much force that my feet leave the ground.

"Thou art a sneaky little shit, Kaspar Lensman," Gunther seethes through clenched teeth. "You adore your sea bitch so much, go to her."

He means to throw me in, to feed me to the mermaid. The mob urges him on, their blood up and hungry for a scapegoat.

"Gunther, don't do this," I plead, eyes on the water for mermaid sign. "I did nothing wrong."

His breath is hot and foul. "You cheated me of the slaughter. Sin enough for me, lad."

Not everyone clamours for my death. My sister pushes through the mob to tear at the harpoonsman, demanding he set me free. Pip springs onto Gunther's back and clamps his teeth onto the man's neck like a lamprey. Bryn is pulled away, Pip shaken off like a gadfly.

Cornelius, the Prefect, orders Gunther to stop and councilman Clovis also objects, telling Gunther that this is not our way. Gunther is deaf to all of it until one voice adds to the protests.

"Put him down, Gunther," his wife pleads. "We've had enough death as it is. No more. Please."

The smolder in the man's eyes drifts into hesitancy, then bewilderment at Agnet's protest. Gunther is clearly not used to hearing objections from his bride, and it has knocked his anger askew. Enough, at least, that he sets me down. Agnet Guiscard has saved my miserable neck. My childish phantasy of rescuing her has been turned on its head.

I almost thank the brute for sparing me.

No one is minding the water, none see the ripples on the waves, but everyone present is drenched in seawater when the creature erupts from below.

Clovis, the councilman who had tried to save my life, is snatched away by webbed fingers, screaming in unholy terror as he is dragged below.

A thunder of pounding feet as everyone stampedes from the pier. No one looks back until they are safely on dry land. Another bloom of red foam kisses the surface of the water and then it is gone. A single shoe bobs to the surface like a toy sailboat.

Gunther the Brave spits and walks off in disgust. His sycophants follow. The rest of the people fix their gaze on me, yoking Clovis's death around my worthless neck. I look away and bury my face in my hands.

I listen to their footfalls drift away. When I sit up, everyone is gone save my siblings. Bryndis looks out at the water while Pip hugs his scrawny knees to his chest. Both of their eyes are puffy with tears.

Pip wipes his nose. "I'm sorry I told on you."

"It's all right. Dry your eyes now."

The desperation in my sister's eyes is something I have not seen before. The intensity of it frightens me.

"What are we going to do?" she asks. "They hate us now."

My head is too empty to reply. I look out over the pier, the shoreline. Everyone has gone home.

"What happened to Agnet?"

Bryndis's face pinches into anger. "God, Kaspar!" she spits and walks away. "Why must you be so selfish?"

# 14

FATHER RETREATS INTO the vestry and will not come out. Bryndis scrapes the dregs of saltcod from the last barrel. There is no more, she says. None of us venture past our gate. Pip vanishes at one point. I find him inside the church, praying to our dead mother's spirit to save us. My blighted hand is now completely numb.

The creature maintains her vigil, keeping us all landlocked. Yesterday morning, Gunhild's cows are found dead in the pasture. Not a mark on either of them. Another dog is found floating in the bay.

A pounding on the door startles us all. I open it to find Ulric bowing, hand on the pommel of his sword.

"The men are meeting at the hall," he says.

"My father does not wish to be disturbed."

His scowl deepens. "He's no use to us. We need you. Come."

"Me?"

Ulric becomes impatient. "Gunther said he needs a steady oarsman. Hurry, now."

Bryndis shakes her head, warning me not to go. I've half a mind to agree, but refusing might prove worse. I take my jacket from the peg and follow the veteran fisherman.

The hall is dim and smoky from the fire. The fishermen huddle around the hearth in their rancid clothes and grim faces. A few are well into their cups, but most are frighteningly sober.

Gunther strides the boards, rallying the men into action. He has a knack for stirring the blood of his fellows.

"We have to take the fight to it," he roars. "The creature has left us no other option. We must fight. We have let this thing unman us for too long. No more of this sitting on our hands and dithering over what to do. We kill the damn thing!"

"But how?" says a voice in the smoky darkness.

"I won't lie to you," the burly man goes on. "This will be a hard fight and some of us may not return. But we have to do it now, before we are too starved and weak to do anything. Every man, every boat. Every blade. Who's with me?"

Fists thump the tables in response, cups spilling liquor.

But the voice in the darkness is not satisfied. "You still haven't said how, Gunther. The serpent will slaughter us all."

The men cease stomping. They murmur, scratch themselves, glance about at their fellow conspirators.

Gunther stares down every pair of eyes in the hall. Mine included. "What are we fighting? It's a damn fish, isn't it? And how do we catch fish?"

"A net!"

"A harpoon!"

Gunther's hand rises to stop them. "With the right bait," he announces. His gaze rolls back to me. "Ulric, if you please?"

The old fisherman is fast, and he is strong, trapping my arms. Cornelius has a burlap sack in his hand. It comes down over my head and everything goes dark.

\*\*\*

My wrists are lashed. I am marched outside, stumbling along blind with the others clamoring around me. The sound of the waves and the thud of men climbing into boats. Oars dipping into water. Echoing across the harbor is the thunder of Gunther's voice, urging his men to watch for signs and be ready with their lances.

The hood is plucked away, and I squint against the

sunlight. Gunther leers down at me, the scar on his cheek white in the sunshine. There is a scaling knife in his hand.

"Time to do your duty, lad," he says. "Bring your sweetheart to us."

"Gunther, stop. Don't do this."

His grin is obscene. "We all have a part to play, Kaspar. Be a man now, by being a worm."

He laughs at his own joke as he cuts the rope from my wrists. Then he pushes me in. Salty darkness and a low hum inside my ears. A cold so sharp it stings like nettles. I kick my legs and flail, but I do not know which way is up. Am I scratching to the surface or clawing my way to the kelp bed?

Without warning I break the waterline, saltwater burning my throat. I look for shore but cannot find it. There are five skiffs on the water, the men stone-faced and gripping their steel. The fishing boats come about to block my path and pen me in. My injured hand is as dead as a stump, making it difficult to tread water.

"For God's sakes, Gunther," I call out with a splash of saltwater on my tongue. "Do you want me to drown?"

He stands tall in his sloop, one boot on the rail. "I'd prefer you to lure the fish in, but a good drowning will suffice."

My wet clothes are heavy, and they tug me down. Did someone put stones in my pockets before throwing me in? How soon before I can't keep my head up and just slip away?

I flail in the chop and Gunther the Brave laughs. "Here, use this to keep your head above water," he says.

A length of wood splashes near me. I lunge after it to stay afloat, only to see the initials carved into the old wood. I look up to see Gunther glaring me down like a gargoyle on a church spire.

He knows. He knows and I am doomed. Whether the mermaid gets me or I drown, it doesn't really matter. Either way, I will not set foot on dry land again.

The cry goes up. It is Gunther's oarsman, Osk, who spots her.

"Yonder she comes! Hard north!"

My brains go numb at the terror coming at me, unseen and unknowable in those blue depths. I have seen what it can do, and I am terrified.

The men tense, nets at the ready, lances gripped in white-knuckled fists. With the vessels blocking my view, I cannot track the creature's approach. The sea is calm, water lapping gently on the hulls. The oarsmen pull and counter the oars to maintain the ring around me.

"She's gone under!" Gunther bellows. "Steady, now."

A gentle splash. I turn and she is here, her strange double-lidded eyes dip at the waterline. I cannot see her mouth, cannot tell if she is smiling or opening her jaws to bite down. I don't want to die, not like this. I brace myself for the coming pain, for the venom of her bite.

Neither occurs. The mermaid does not strike, her gaze inscrutable and foreign. I cannot tell if she is amused or enraged. Of the harpoonists and their spears, she either does not see them or is not alarmed by their presence. I hear the voices of the fishermen puzzle at her behavior.

"Why doesn't it eat him?" says one.

Another responds. "The stupid boy has made a pet of it. Look at it."

The creature circles slowly, her strange eyes fixed on me. The first net is flung, then the first harpoon. The maiden slips below easily and surfaces behind me. More nets, another lance. Again, she eludes the fishermen's weapons. The sail of her dorsal fins twinkles with sunlight as it cuts the surface. It is toying with me the way a cat bats a mouse before biting its head off.

"Why won't it go for him?" says a voice.

"Maybe she prefers the taste of men to boys," another replies.

I glance at Gunther. He has yet to fire his harpoon. Eyes on the water, he is studying the way she darts and feints to avoid capture. Tracking her locomotion, anticipating her moves.

"Maybe Kaspar is secretly a girl," laughs long-nosed Sligo.

A sharp tug on my ankle pulls me below. I catch only a murky vision of the mermaid gliding past me before I claw to the surface. Spitting out the spume, I see a net whirl over me with precise aim. Then Gunther's harpoon sails from his powerful arm.

He has timed it correctly. Tangled in the net, she spins and bucks at it, but does not see the harpoon coming. It drives into her ribs with enough force to knock her back and my eardrums split at her shrieks of pain.

The sea boils as she spins and flails. Sea spray drenches the men as they cast more nets and fling their spears. The spray blooms red with her blood.

The churning stops and the water stills. The men hurrah in victory and Gunther barks at them to reel in his catch. Hand-over-hand, they draw their harpoon lines to bring the prize to the surface. Looking into the water, I can see a hazy form grow as it rises directly under me. It slithers between my legs like a lover and breaks topside, her belly rolling to the sun. The men keep pulling, dragging their vessels closer to their catch. To a man, they all sport a hungry, greedy fire in their eyes.

It is all a ruse. She rights herself, locks eyes on me for a single heartbeat, and then dives hard below. Three men are jerked clean into the water. One boat pitches badly and overturns at the violence of her plunge. Gunther hacks his tow line with a machete and screams at the others to do the same before she pulls them all under.

The men in the water, Sligo and Horst, and another man I do not know, swim for the nearest boat. Their fellows try to haul them in, only to have each man ripped from their hands. The water roils like a boiling cauldron and the men in the water cry out in terror at the thing circling beneath them. Each one shrieks, bobbing in their own blood as the monster ravages them. Gunther fires another harpoon at the creature and Ulric slashes the water with his cutlass, but both are powerless to stop the slaughter. The screams of the dying men cease as severed limbs and bloodied torsos roll to the surface.

I swim for the pier with the curses of the fishermen in my ears as they stab and slash impotently at the water. One skiff is capsized, and another punctured through the hull, sinking quickly. These men wail in terror as they join their comrades in the red surf. Yet one vessel skims past me as I drive hard for the dock.

Gunther thunders at Osk and Brom to row like hell because the very devil herself is coming for their souls. The sloop is almost to the pier when a torrent of spray erupts under them, sending all three into the drink. I cannot see them flailing in the chop, but I hear their agonized screams as the creature goes after them. I claw the waves like a madman until I feel solid stone in my grip.

The townsfolk crowd the dock, their faces white as they witness the slaughter. They fling ropes into the sea and reach to pluck their sailors out. Distracted thus, no one sees my approach or lowers a helping hand. I see Agnet screaming on the dock as her husband's boat is destroyed. I call to her, but she does not hear me. I pant on the stone and watch as her husband and his oarsmen are plucked from the water and dragged up onto the pier. There is blood everywhere and their mewls of agony fill my ears until each is carried away. I see a severed head bob on the waves. Sligo, the man betrothed to my sister. His outlandish nose is upright like a sail.

The sky darkens and a briny chill creeps into my bones. I sit up and look out at the destruction rising and falling on the waves in the bay. Splintered wood and capsized hulls, the useless nets and the broken bodies of the fishermen. All of it floating in the chop. The gulls cry and flap as they peck at an easy meal.

And out there on the water reigns the sea maiden who has all but wiped out our fleet in a single afternoon. I swear to God she looks right at me as she devours the floating remains of the fishermen. No other soul is plucked from the sea this day and the mermaid leaves nothing left of the dead to bury.

# 15

I SHIVER THE rest of the day, unable to rid the chill from my bones no matter how close I huddle by the fire. Our home has become grim. Father remains locked in the vestry, oblivious to the attempt of the fishermen to murder his own son. Bryndis will not speak to me, clanging the pots and bashing the board as she scrapes whatever scraps we have left into a thin stew. Pip is singing songs about the mermaid, gibberish nonsense about how prettily she swims and how green her locks are. I tell him to stop, but he will not, so I shove him in the larder and turn the latch. Rhymes leak out from under the door in his thin voice.

All feeling is gone from my left hand. It is a leprous, blackened thing that I do not recognize. I can move my fingers, but the creature's venom has confounded every nerve. There is no sensation to it at all. Slipping the knife from my belt, I prick the blackened skin with the blade, drawing out the dark blood, but there is no pain. The fingernails have become loose and when I press on them, a foul-smelling puss oozes out from the cuticles. It is revolting.

I try not to recall the midwife's warning that I may have to lop the diseased limb off. When a knock on the door startles me, I slip the foul thing back into my shirt to hide it.

Magda stops in to check on us, bringing news. Osk and Brom are unharmed, although badly shaken by what they have endured. Gunther the Brave lives, but just barely. Both of his legs were sheared off by the creature's teeth, along with his left arm. Magda had spoken to the midwife after she had bandaged his wounds. Gunther is strong, Hagar said, and will most likely survive, but alas, what manner of life will he have now? I ask about Agnet, which earns a nasty glare from my sister. I ignore it. Magda informs me that Gunther's wife has gone silent. She helped wrap the wounds, fetching water when the midwife asked, but the girl was mute as a stone.

"The poor thing," Magda concludes with a slow shake of her head. "Heartbroken into silence."

"Now married to a stump," I reply. My neighbor and my sister both wince at my poor taste.

"I am sorry to hear about Sligo." Magda pats my sister's knee in condolence. "He was an adequate fellow."

"Thank you," Bryndis replies. With Sligo dead, she is free, but I cannot tell if this makes her happy. Her face is stony all the time now. "It is tragic."

"Although, perhaps not the best match for you," says our neighbor. Since Mother's disappearance, Magda has been especially kind to us all. She thinks quite highly of Bryndis. "How is young Calder? Has he been by to offer his sympathies?"

Bryndis' voice is as flat as her eyes. "I saw him in the square yesterday. He acted like he didn't know me."

"Silly boy," Magda replies. "He'll come round."

The wind picks up, whistling down the chimney and pushing the door open. Magda says she doesn't like the sound of it and fears something bad is blowing in off the sea.

"Bad omens," I say, securing the door. "How could it get any worse?"

Perhaps this question provoked the fates, for not a minute later comes a hubbub of disturbance. Some fool is yammering down the laneway and another is crying out near the pier. I open the door, craning an ear to catch what the fuss is about.

Something, shriek the voices, is crawling out of the sea.

We run to the docks, expecting to see the mermaid herself flopping and wriggling on dry land, but she is not the cause of the ruckus. Something dark and glistening is creeping up over the edge of the wharf and slithering in a great mass toward us.

Beasts of the sea, in all shapes and sizes. There are octopus and crabs, starfish and sea urchins, along with countless other creatures that I cannot identify. Thousands of them, slithering and swarming all along the shoreline. Onward they come, unfolding tentacles and clawing with pincers, like an invading army laying siege to our village. It is a revolting sight. A few people try to sweep them back or stomp them underfoot, but there are too many and they just keep coming, crawling up the wharf into town. It is as if the sea has declared war on us and its barbarian horde is determined to storm our gates.

Pip wades barefoot into the squirming mess until Bryndis pulls him away, insisting we run home. Magda blasphemes the name of our Lord, horrified at the invading mass. When a large snow crab scuttles close, I snatch it from the ground.

My sister makes a sour face. "Put it back, Kaspar."

"Look at the size of it," I say, holding it carefully to avoid the snapping pincers. "This will feed us all tonight."

"Are you daft?" says Magda. "The mermaid sent it. It is probably poisonous. Get rid of it."

A tug-of-war plays out between my empty belly and my brains. I toss it back and we all hurry home, locking our doors like Magda suggests.

*** 

No one sleeps. The sound of this invading force is unrelenting outside the window; the awful squirming, sucking, squishing racket of it all. When the sun rises, the townsfolk step out of their doors to find the streets overwhelmed with the damned things. There is nowhere to step without squishing an octopus or cracking a shell. What mad suicide mission was this? The creatures have crawled into town only to die on the cobbles. The smell of it is noxious, and it will only get worse as the day warms. Everywhere I look, men are shoveling the rotting things like snow in winter. The women broom the creepers from their stoops, but there are too many and there is nowhere to put them. Raking them all out to sea will take days.

I scan the bay, expecting to see the mermaid patrolling the harbor, but she is not there. The sea is calm and dappled with sunlight. The gulls have arranged themselves on the pier in an unnatural silence. Why are they not scavenging the veritable feast that lies in stinking heaps on every street? Perhaps they instinctively know the smell of evil and will not touch the dead creatures. Some of the villagers are not so wise, having cooked a crab or roasted a squid. These foolhardy souls are now green in their sickbeds, poisoned by the delicacies.

My shoes are slippery with gore by the time I make it across town to the drab little cottage with the damaged roof. A thin trickle of smoke rises from the chimney. I kick the starfish from the step and knock on the door. I no longer care who will see me or what they will say. I suppose I could claim that I am here to ask after Gunther's health. *What a good lad that Kaspar is*, they will say. *Inquiring about our brave harpoonsman, even after Gunther tried to murder him.* There are times when I long for a match to burn this entire village down.

I am giggling over the thought when Agnet opens the door. She does not look surprised or happy to see me. Her eyes are lifeless, the mouth drawn thin. She is only sixteen, but she seems to have aged twenty years in a single night. When her eyes fall to the stinking sea creatures fouling her yard, she betrays no reaction.

"Yes?" she says, as if I am a stranger.

"Agnet." My tongue stalls, becomes stone. Coming up the path, I was bursting with a thousand things to say to her. Now my head is as empty as a shell.

"What is it, Kaspar?"

"I came to see if you were all right. And Gunther, too. I was worried."

This last part is not a complete lie. I hope that he has died in the night.

Her voice is as flat as her eyes. "I see."

Is she drunk? I have never seen her like this. "May I come in?"

"This is not a good time."

"I won't stay long. Please."

She moves aside and I come through. I have never stepped foot inside Gunther's cottage before, although I have often tried to picture it in my mind. Or rather, I pictured Agnet inside it. What she was doing at any moment, or if she was happy. The interior is dark, and it smells of woodsmoke and fish. Mounted over the hearth is the sailfin of the swordfish that tried to pluck out Gunther's eye. A net is draped over a chair, waiting to be mended.

There is a bad smell and an even worse sound coming from the bed on the far side of the room. A curtain hangs from the rafters for privacy. I almost do not recognize Gunther's voice, moaning and mumbling in pain. Restless in his torment, I can hear him creaking the bed and swishing the sheets.

"How is he?"

Her eyes go to the curtain and then turn away. "Like this. The pain has made him senseless, but it won't let him sleep."

No wonder her eyes are so blasted. I have had only a taste of his moaning and I want to run away. How could she have endured this all night? How much longer will it continue?

"I'm sorry, Agnet." I scrounge for something to console her. "I hear the midwife believes he will survive."

"His pride keeps his heart beating," she says. "Last night, when the pain abated, he told me he would not let a woman murder him like this. He even vowed revenge."

"Sit down," I say, as if I am the host here. She drops into a chair. "You must be exhausted. Is there anyone who can help you?"

Another tortured cry rises from the sickbed. It makes me

cringe, but Agnet betrays no reaction. I suppose she is numb to it by now.

She rubs at a callous on her cracked hands. "How could I ask someone else to endure that?"

"I'm sorry," I say again.

The fire pops softly. A spindle falls from a shelf and rolls to our feet. Agnet picks it up and turns it idly in her hand.

She lowers her voice. "I heard he tried to kill you. That he used you for bait. Is that true?"

"He needed to lure her close so he could deliver the killing blow."

She says nothing, turning the spindle over and over. I don't know why I am making excuses for him. When I reach for her hand, she recoils like I'm leprous.

"He knows," I say.

"He knows what?"

"He knows."

Her eyes finally come to life, dilating with terror. Her chapped lips curl into a sneer. "How? Did you boast?"

Her gaze is too hot, and I cannot meet it. "Our initials," I tell her. "I threw it into the sea. What are the chances that it would wash up at his feet?"

The spindle becomes still. Her eyes drop to the floor. "He's been acting strangely of late. Accusing me of being unfaithful."

"But, you haven't. That was all before you married."

"Do you think that matters to him? His pride will not accept it."

The moaning from the sickbed does not stop. I stifle a wicked urge to bark at the man to shut up. I doubt he even knows I am here.

"Father keeps some brandy hidden away in the tabernacle. He thinks no one knows. I'll fetch it. It might ease his pain."

Agnet slumps, letting her hair fall to hide her face. If there are tears, I do not see them. I only hear the hitch of a sob catch her throat.

"What am I going to do, Kaspar? He cannot even walk, let alone fish. We'll starve. I am chained to him."

She does not pull away this time when I take her hand. How rough they are now, worked to the bone. One fingernail is purple.

"We will find a way," I tell her.

"Stop it. That foolishness will get us both killed."

My voice breaks. "Why do you talk to me this way? I have never stopped loving you." I shake a hand at the curtain. "Despite all this, I could not stop. Have you?"

"Keep your voice down."

A roar bellows from the other side of the curtain, raw-voiced and angry. "Who's there? Agnet? Agnet, damn you! Who is there?"

We both rise. I promise to bring the brandy and leave. At the cottage's little gate, I slip on a rotting squid and fall hard, a spiny urchin stinging my backside.

***

By midday, the stench is unbearable. People go to and fro with kerchiefs pressed to their noses to ward off the smell of the sea life rotting on the cobbles. I spend the morning scavenging for food. Sigga, the miller's daughter, is willing to trade a sack of meal for the last coin I have. It is a paltry score, as the meal is fuzzed with mold, but it will put something in our bellies. I return to the church to find my sister pounding on the door of the vestry.

"Will he not come out?"

"He's locked himself in," Bryndis replies. Her hand is red from the hammering. "He won't even answer me."

"Why waste your time? Leave him," I say, crossing to the tabernacle at the altar.

"He has duties. All those men need a burial."

"The creature left nothing to bury."

Her eyes narrow in disgust. "They still require a proper funeral. A benediction or something."

Reaching into the tabernacle, I scrounge around for the

hidden flask. There is the chalice and a hymnal, but no flask, no wine skin.

"What are you doing?"

"Where is father's brandy?"

Bryndis wags her chin at the locked door. "Probably in there, with him. Why?"

"For Gunther. He's out of his mind in pain."

"Kaspar, the man tried to murder you. Why are you helping him?"

"It's not him I'm helping."

Bryndis blows out her cheeks in an exhale and flops into a pew. "For God's sakes, Kaspar. Just leave the girl be."

"How can I? She is all alone, chained to that mewling beast. He's not even a man anymore."

Frustrated, I join her on the pew. The skeleton of the legendary sea monster hangs on the wall before us. The haphazard patchwork of bone and fin looks preposterous in the greasy light of the window.

"Little Tito was taken," she says. "Did you hear?"

A boy of seven, with almost white hair, and five sisters. "Ersham's son? What happened?"

"He was out on the pier with his sisters. They had gone to watch the mermaid. It snatched him from the dock, right out of the hands of his sisters."

"Good God. Now, Ersham has no heir."

"One more funeral that needs doing," she utters, her eyes moving to the locked door of the vestry. "We need to keep an eye on Pip. Keep him away from the water."

"I doubt she'd go for him. No meat on his bones."

She doesn't find this amusing. "I'm serious. Tito was with his five sisters. It took only him, not the girls."

I agree to her precautions. Her eyes fall to the sack I bartered from Sigga.

"What's this?"

"Fish meal. It's all I could find."

Bryndis unties the drawstrings and opens the sack. Her nose turns up at the smell. "It's gone bad."

"Scrape off the moldy layer. Some of it will still be good."

The conversation withers, much like our dwindling prospects. High up on the wall, the eyeless sockets of the sea monster gather dust.

Stepping into the yard, we find Pip with his hands in a pail of seawater. Tongue extended, he toils at some strange task.

Our sister is already annoyed with him. "What are you doing now, Pip?"

His face lights up at us. "Kaspar, I have something for you. Come and close your eyes."

"Not now."

"Come quick!"

I only indulge the little twerp because denying him will make it worse. He tells me to take a knee and close my eyes.

"I have made you a crown, Kaspar," he says. "The most wonderful crown of them all."

"I see. It is my coronation day, is it?"

"Glory be," he says, placing something on my head.

It is wet and it smells bad. It also squirms like it's alive. When Bryndis squeals in disgust, I shake it off. There on the ground lies a ring of small starfish, stitched together with a needle and thread. The creatures writhe and twist, dying in the open air.

Revolted, I shove the little turnip away. Pip flops onto his backside, hurt.

"Don't you like it?"

I storm into the rectory. "What is wrong with you?"

Bryndis shakes her head at our disturbed little brother. "Told you he wouldn't like it."

Thousands of them, slithering and swarming all along the shoreline.
Onward they come, unfolding tentacles and clawing with pincers,
like an invading army laying siege to our village.

# 16

THE FISH MEAL is rancid, but we force it down. Pip leaves a bowl outside the vestry for father. When supper is over, Magda knocks on our door to ask if we have any tobacco to spare. Bryndis finds a pouch of it on the mantle. Magda fills her clay pipe and tells us that the mermaid has taken another lad. Cleto, a boy of fifteen, was snatched from the beach at sundown.

"How awful," Bryndis remarks. The boy in question had once tried to woo my sister, but Bryndis disliked his stringy hair and hangdog face.

The flame of the match dips as Magda lights the pipe. "The men won't go near the water now. Most are hiding in their huts or gone uphill to the trees."

Pip watches the smoke drift to the rafters. "Hugo took his family and left."

This is news to all of us. "Left how?" I say.

"Up the mountain," Pip squeaks, wiping his nose. "He said they would take their chances."

The mountains that surrounded our village are nigh impassible. The trail, if one can call it that, is littered with the bones of those who lost the path or were caught unprepared by a winter storm. Only the desperate would attempt it. Hugo and his wife, Laufa, have five children. Three of them under the age of eight.

We all bow our heads when Magda offers a quick prayer for their souls.

I hold my good hand to the hearth to warm it and recall

94

the hands of the mermaid, the strange webbing between her fingers.

"Do you think it will ever go away?"

Magda looks at me. "The sea maiden? Hard to say."

"Is it going to eat us all?" Pip wants to know.

"No, no." Our neighbor pats Pip's misshapen head to comfort him. "I think Hagar's claim is the most likely. It came into the bay on the full moon. It will escape on the next one."

Pip sniffles. "When will that be?"

"Tomorrow."

That seems to lift my brother's spirits. Mine, also, to be honest. We fall silent for a spell, watching the flames lick the hearth. The smell of Magda's pipe fills the room.

Bryndis stiffens, sits up straight. "What is that sound?"

"It's lovely, whatever it is," Magda agrees.

All I hear is the crackle of the fire. "What sound?"

"That voice," Bryndis says. She opens the door. "Someone is singing."

Magda shuffles to her side, craning an ear. "Is it Roslyn? She has a beautiful voice, that one."

"I've never heard Roslyn sing like that," Bryndis replies. "My God, listen to it."

I hear nothing from the open door. The perpetual sound of the surf, but that is all. I ask Pip if he hears the singing, but he seems as baffled as I am. Are the women delusional? The moon is almost full, and it casts a strong throw over the bay, waves rippling in its light. When something cuts through the moonlight twinkle of the waves, it becomes apparent to all where the singing is coming from.

"Get back inside," I say, slamming the door and locking it. I order Pip to close the shutters on the windows. "Don't listen to it. Cover your ears if you have to."

Neither of them do as they're told. Our neighbor and my sister return to their seats at the hearth and continue to listen. Bryndis tucks her hair behind an ear and her eyes take on a dreamy sheen that leaves me with no good feeling.

Pip sneezes, three consumptive bellows that leave him dizzy. A string of yellow phlegm wiggles on his chin. When Bryndis spasms in an abrupt shiver, the haze melts from her eyes.

"It's gone now," she says.

***

The church is quiet. It holds only one soul this night, and that is mine. The cold flagstones and smell of the wooden pews are comforting. I light a candle under the icon of Torgrim the Unbending and wonder if the fabled hero will return from beyond the grave to save us again. On the lectern sits the parish registry, open to the latest page. Father must have forgotten it out here.

I run a finger down the last names listed in the ledger. Names of all the dead men, along with the date and means of death. For each cause, Father has written "taken by God." The ink pot and the quill are here so I dip the nib into the ink to amend his record. Crossing out the word 'God', I scribble down the word 'mermaid'. There, the record stands accurate now. I wonder if Father will notice. In his current state, he doesn't seem to notice anything.

When my blasphemy is done, I go to a pew and pray. I pray to the Almighty to save our souls, to make the creature go back to the open seas. I pray for Agnet to be returned to me, for us to be together like we used to. I pray for her to be safe.

The prayer is ended when I genuflect to the four points of the compass. The stern countenance of the One True God, carved out of ancient oak, hangs just below the brittle skeleton of the sea monster. Two dead gods, two corpses hung for display. Is either real? I wonder which one I am praying to. Are both deaf or has one craned its ear to my whispers? When a fragment of sea monster bone falls to the floor, I wonder if I have doomed us all.

***

The wrack of octopus and starfish on our streets has

putrefied into a sludge under the rays of the sun. It clings to shoes and makes the cobbles slippery. The stinking fumes ripple like heat from the pathways. The women go about their tasks, kerchiefs pressed to their noses against the miasma. There is nary a man in sight. I see Ulric standing in the doorway of his hovel, as if unwilling to step beyond his threshold. He tells me that Gunther's oarsmen, Osk and Brom, have both disappeared in the night. They were last seen on the eastern wharf, clumsy with drink, and singing bawdy songs to the creature that had mutilated their skipper. They had raised their fists in anger, cursing the monster and pissing into the sea to underwrite their contempt. Late this morning, Brom's head is found washed up on the beach by two little girls. His eyes are gone and a small crab has made a nest of the empty socket. No part of Osk is found.

I spend the bulk of another day foraging but have nothing to show for it. With our coins all spent, I pry gems from the chalice to trade, but no one will barter with me. As the family of the village parson, we had once held some prominence in town, but all that is gone. We have been reduced to paupers. Life is difficult under normal circumstances here, and beggars do not survive long in our precious little hamlet on the sea.

The atmosphere in town is strung tauter than a tourniquet. Neighbor accuses neighbor of stealing eggs or sacks of meal. Friend turns on friend over who or what is truly to blame for the sea monster terrorizing the harbor. There are strange sights, too. Gnud, the miller's son, and Hafdan, the soft-headed son of the blacksmith, are both clad in their sister's frocks and bonnets. I thought they were playing some strange game, but when I see another boy in a dress, I learn the truth. Fearing for their son's lives, mother's have taken to dressing their boys as girls to hide them from the mermaid.

Boys dressed in frocks. Men hiding at home while the women go about. Our little world has turned upside-down.

I pass by Gunther's cottage and rap on the door. It opens a few inches, Agnet's face half-shadowed in the gap. She looks even more trampled than before. Her husband's moans leak through the gap in the door.

"Agnet, are you all right?"

The color in her eyes has faded to a sickly shade. Whatever spark that once animated them is now snuffed out. "What do you want?"

"I was worried about you."

"You can't just come knocking," she says. "Someone will see."

"Does that matter anymore?" I gesture to the village behind me. "The whole place has gone mad."

The bellowing voice inside the cottage rises to a fevered pitch, desperate and terrified. It sounds nothing like Gunther the Brave. He howls for someone named Solda to help him, to save him. Agnet flinches at every rise in his pitch.

"Who is Solda?"

"Isolde," she says. "His first wife."

I never liked the woman. She was unpleasant and never spoke a kind word to anyone. Something crashes inside the cottage, like a dish hurled against a wall. Gunther's tone alters, along with his words. He screams Agnet's name this time. She has no choice but to go to him. I grasp at straws, holding on by my fingernails.

"Tell me what to do. How do I help you?"

Her eyes remain on the ground, refusing to meet mine. "There is nothing you can do, Kaspar. Go home."

I go home. What else am I to do? Slopping through the muck of liquefying jellyfish and mollusks, I think back to my foolish daydreams of rescuing Agnet from the ogre who holds her prisoner. My face reddens at how childish they seem now. How indulgent. The romantic flights of a brainless boy.

Bryndis startles when I slam the door behind me. She is at the table, head down on the board.

"What's wrong?"

She raises her head, but there are no tears. Her expression is null.

"Calder is missing," she says.

Her sweetheart. "What happened?"

"Magda said he went down to the wharf with a crossbow, barking about revenge. No one has seen him since."

"I'm sorry, Bryn."

"Did you find anything to eat?"

"No."

Bryndis lays her head back down on the table.

"Where is Father?"

Her hand points to the church. "Still in the vestry."

Marching into the church, I hammer at the vestry door and demand that he come out. There is no answer. I storm out to the yard, where the ax lies sunk into the cutting stump. I pluck it out, march back inside, and chop at the thick door. Bryndis orders me to stop and Pip flaps about like some crazed squirrel, screeching at me to put the ax away. On the other side of the door comes our father's voice, yowling to be left alone.

The wood splinters. The latch snaps away and falls to the floor. I kick the door open and wince at the smell. Father sits at his scribing table looking like the prophet Ptolemaeus, driven mad by his own sacred texts. Bloodshot eyes and blotchy skin, a thin skein of drool running into his filthy beard. When he admonishes me for destroying his door, I hold the ax high enough to lop his head clean off. He backs away, scurrying into the corner.

"Your brandy. Where is it?"

He doesn't answer me. Instead, he puts his hands together and prays for God to strike me down.

I pull the drawers from the desk and shake the contents to the floor. I sweep every book from the shelf, but no bottle materializes.

"Where did you hide it? Tell me!"

My father slinks away like a crab caught out in the

daylight. None of us are allowed inside the vestry. This is my first glimpse of his inner sanctum, his Holy-of-Holies. A framed picture sits high on a shelf. A simple cameo profile of a young woman. I recognize the shape of that impudent nose immediately. Our lost mother. I push it aside and hidden behind it lies the brownglass bottle of brandy.

The bottle slips into my pocket. I take down the cameo and trace a finger along the contours of mother's nose and chin. Father mutters at me not to touch it with my filthy hands, to put it back and go away.

When father scolds me a second time, I turn and kick him. Then I kick him again until he cowers like an orphaned child. I squat down to his level and hold the portrait to his face.

"What did you do to her? Did she really jump into the sea to get away from you?"

He covers his ears and looks away. I snatch his rancid beard to make him look at me.

"Did you dump her in the bay after you murdered her? Tell me."

"No, no, no," he gibbers. His eyes are crazed. "She is here. She has come back to us."

I hear Pip behind me, pleading with me to leave Father alone. I ignore him. I shake my father like a rag, like a babe that won't stop crying.

"She swims the bay now," he says. "She's an angel, sent to protect us from these terrible people. These brutes, these heathens."

His mind has snapped. Pip keeps begging me to stop, to let Father be.

I feel something wicked bloom inside my chest, like mold blackening an overripe apple. The ax remains in the corner where I stood it against the wall. What is the cost of patricide? How damned is one's soul for murdering their own father? I imagine there must be a special grotto of scorching hellfire for us.

As much as I want to, I cannot bring the ax down on his pathetic head. Pip runs to Father, shielding him with his scrawny frame.

"This is all your fault, Kaspar," says my sister. She buries her face in her hands and cries.

"How is this my fault?"

The look in her eyes is withering. "The mermaid. You summoned her."

I have half a mind to bring the ax down on her skull. "Are you insane? I did no such thing."

"The night you put flower petals under your pillow," she says. "That's what brought the luremaid to us. I told you not to do it, but you wouldn't listen."

Has everyone lost their minds? I storm out of the vestry with the brandy and drop the ax in the yard. I go through the gate with half-remembered fables swimming in my thoughts. The storybook tales mother used to tell, about knights rescuing princesses from dungeons.

# 17

I RUN ACROSS TOWN, splashing through the putrid sludge with my sister's accusation ringing my ears. I push it away, refusing to even consider such a ludicrous idea. By the time I reach the cottage, my eyes are watering from the stench. I bang on the door, calling Agnet's name. Across the lane, I see her neighbor step outside to see what the fuss is about. The old woman sees me and goes back inside. I hammer on the door again.

Why won't she answer? Is Agnet hiding on the other side, wishing I will go away? Has something happened to her?

The latch is old. It falls open at a slight push.

Agnet is not here. The cottage is small enough to see everything in one sweep, save for the bed behind the screen. The hearth is cold. The only sound in the room is the buzzing of the flies swarming against the window. There is none of the agonized moaning or mewling I heard on my previous visits. Has Gunther been moved elsewhere, or has he died? Perhaps his legs grew back, and he left, dancing a jig?

With Agnet gone, I am robbed of the gratitude that I was anticipating. A gesture of thanks, an embrace even. I hang my head at my own pettiness. My sister is right; I am a selfish cabbage. I clear a spot on the table, pushing aside the hemp and the awls used for repairing nets. I set the bottle of brandy on the cleared table so that Agnet will notice it when she returns. There is no point leaving a note. Agnet will know where the mysterious brandy has come from. Her grateful embrace will simply be postponed.

A stirring comes from behind the curtain. A low groan like the grinding of oyster shells. I draw back the curtain and look down on the catastrophe that was once our heroic fisherman.

Gunther the Brave is a giant of a man, with massive arms and a broad chest. His injuries have rendered him half that now, more ghost than man. His skin is sallow and beaded with a greasy sweat. Where his legs had been, there are now only stumps wrapped in coarse bandages. The blood has stained the linen to a blackish color and foul maggots writhe within its folds. Another dressing is applied to the left arm where the limb has been cleaved off. The bandages here ooze a dark, jelly-like substance. His cock, which Gunther constantly boasted of, is a worm shriveled into its nest of hair.

Worst of all, however, is Gunther's face. Gone is the anger and the pride that had always animated his features. His mouth is open, the eyes shrunken and terrified as if he is witnessing some terrible vision on the ceiling above. A gurgling hiss rattles from his throat.

My mouth is dry. "Gunther? Can you hear me?"

His eyes wheel about until they find me. Even this small action seems painful.

I fetch the bottle from the table and hold it up for him to see. "I brought some brandy. For the pain."

I think he understands. His eyes focus, become clear.

With a small flourish, I pull the cork and raise the bottle in a salute to his health. Then I guzzle down a hearty swallow of the stuff and stick the cork back.

Confusion clouds his darting eyes as I set the bottle aside. The bafflement drains into fear when I take the pillow from under his head. If the brave fisherman had but a fraction of his fabled strength, he would hurl me across the room. As it is, his one hand paws at mine like a weak kitten. I throw my weight against the pillow to stifle him, but still he thrashes. The stump of his severed arm wiggles up and down like a puppy dog's tail. His body twists and flails, the bandages coming undone. Blood and worms spill over the bed sheet. I hear him mewling through the pillow. Is he calling out for Agnet or for his first wife, Isolde?

Smothering the life out of him takes a long time. My arms are limp from the effort of it when it is finally over. I lift the pillow away. His mouth gapes open, the eyes bald and bloodshot. If terror has a face, here it is.

"Who's the hero now, Gunther?"

I want to feel exultant over this, but that is not to be. I feel nothing, in fact. Neither remorse nor triumph. I have despised Gunther with everything I have, but now that he is dead, that anger dissipates like smoke. I tell myself that I have been merciful by putting the harpooner out of his misery. I have freed Agnet from a life of grovelling poverty caring for half a husband. I want to feel like a hero from the old sagas, but what have I really accomplished here? I have smothered a cripple. It is no more heroic an act than drowning a kitten.

I draw the curtain, so I do not have to look at him. Settling into a chair, I place the brandy on the table and wait. When Agnet returns, I will break the unfortunate news to her. I will tell her how I had brought the brandy to ease her husband's pain, only to find that I was too late. Poor Gunther has expired in his sickbed. She will be shocked, and she will cry. I will pour Agnet a dram of the brandy to settle her. My arms will hold her, my words will console her in her grief.

When the shock ebbs away, Agnet will dry her eyes and be relieved. She will even be grateful for my shoulder to cry on. I will take her gentle face in my hands and tell her that I will always be hers, that I have never stopped loving her and will cherish her until the day I die.

My knack for phantasy and woolgathering has always been a problem. My father often scolds me for daydreaming the hours away, my work neglected and undone. There are two worlds: the real one and the other that lives inside my head. If only I could stitch one to the other.

Agnet does not return. I don't know how long I have sat here dreaming, but the shadows have grown thick, and a sharp smell is drifting up from behind the curtain. I open the door to find that night has fallen. The sky is clear and dotted with stars so green they glint like emeralds against ink. The moon is strong, washing the village in a silvery haze. Looking up, I see that she is full. A comet arcs past her face, scratching the velvet night with a pale scar that throbs and does not fade.

\*\*\*

Where can she be at this late hour? Agnet is not one to shirk her duties or gallivant about. The only place I can think of is her parent's house, up on the northern rind of the village where the forest begins. I make my way there, careful not to slip in the dark on the evil slime coating the street. Rounding the miller's hut, I see old Ulric standing in his doorway. He seems agitated, and he holds a poker in his fist.

When I call to him, the old fisherman startles and raises the poker like a weapon. "Who's there?"

"Ulric, it's me. Kaspar. What's wrong?"

The poker comes down, but he remains alert. Frightened. "Have you seen Sabine?"

His second daughter, a friend of my sister's. As I come closer, I can see his face better in the light. The old man's lip is swollen and cracked with dried blood.

"What happened?"

"Something has taken my Sabine," he says. His rheumy eyes dart hither and yon, as if he expects an attack from the shadows.

He isn't making sense. "Someone took her? Who?"

"No, no. The girl's bewitched. Not herself. God preserve us."

I touch his arm to calm him, but he flinches. Stumbles back. "Easy, Ulric. Tell me what happened."

"She was sitting by the fire, the darning in her lap, when she became upset and animated about something. She said someone was singing and wasn't it the most glorious sound we had ever heard. I heard nothing. My wife has been deaf for ages, and she heard nothing. Sabine dropped the stocking she'd been mending and went to the door. She said she had to know who was singing like an angel. When I tried to stop her, she became violent. Her eyes were like that of a wild animal. She knocked me to the floor and threatened to do the same to her mother. Can you imagine?"

"What on earth came over her?" I do not know Sabine Dulfgutter well, but she is a mild mouse of a girl.

"She stole my sword," the old man says. He seems to deflate upon telling his tale, leaning against the doorframe to keep himself upright. "Do ye know how many generations that cutlass has been passed down? Sabine said she would gut me with it if I tried to stop her."

"Go rest, Ulric. She'll come back." His wife comes to the door to guide her distraught husband inside.

"Ulric, which way did she go?"

His hand comes up, one gnarled fingerbone pointing south. "There. To the water."

I wonder if Agnet is with Sabine. I thank him and make my way to the wharf. I slip twice, falling once to the rancid slime. When I turn out of the laneway to the open air of the bay, I see them. Agnet is there, along with Sabine, and even my sister. The silver light of the moon flashes, reflecting off the polished cutlass in Sabine's hand.

They are lined up on the pier, every girl in the village. Eyes on the water, they watch the mermaid swim in the moonlight. Although I can hear nothing but the waves lapping the shore, I know that the mermaid is singing, and she is singing only to the assembled daughters of our cursed village.

# 18

THEY KNEEL ON the stone pier, hands folded in their laps as they gaze upon the mermaid in the bay. All silent, all enraptured by a song only they can hear. Some arcane ritual is being performed before my eyes, one that feels both holy and profane. My heart deadens at the sight of Agnet among them. I want to go to her, to bring her away from the others, but I dare not go any closer to the water. Not with the sea-woman out there.

The breeze skimming across the face of the water changes direction, and the girls all stand as one, the way the congregation rises at the conclusion of prayers. There are a few remaining fishing boats still tethered to the dock. I watch Agnet, my sister, and Sabine climb down into the boats and rummage around each vessel. They hand up tools and these are passed around to those waiting on the pier. There is an eerie martial precision to the way they march from the wharf and onto the thoroughfare that leads into town. As they move past my position, I see the tools they have taken from the skiffs. Knives and long hooks, harpoons and a club for braining fish. Sabine holds her father's cutlass, while my sister clutches a machete that I recognized as belonging to Clovis.

Agnet holds an iron hook in her small hand as she falls in line at the end of this silent procession. I creep from my hiding place and take her arm. When she turns, her eyes are not her own, looking at me like she doesn't know who I am.

I keep my voice to a whisper. "What are you doing? Why do you have the hook?"

She says nothing. Her head turns to the procession of girls who are now melting into the shadows. I have to shake her to bring her attention back to me.

"Are you all right? Are you hurt?"

Has she suddenly been struck deaf? Has the mermaid taken her tongue?

"Agnet, listen to me. Something has happened. To Gunther." I am out of breath and tripping on my own words. But she needs to know. "He's dead. I went to check on him, and I found him cold. He suffers no more."

Her reaction is a blink, but nothing more. No surprise, no tears. A lock of her hair falls across her gentle face, so I brush it behind her ear. The moon lights her eyes in a way that reveals something otherworldly and terrifying. This is not my Agnet, this is not the girl I have given my heart to. She is changed.

"Do you hear me? He's gone. You are free."

What has the mermaid done? What enchantment has stolen Agnet's wits along with her tongue? She should be overjoyed to learn she is free from the brute she was forced to wed. I rattle her again, desperate to get through to her, to pierce this enchantment.

"Agnet, you are free. We are free. We can be together now. Without shame, without sin."

Her reaction is that of someone stepping barefoot onto a hot coal. She tears her arm from my grip.

"What have you done?" Her eyes light up, but not in a kind way. "What have you done, Kaspar?"

I bungle a response. This is not going how I want it to. "I did what needed doing. It was merciful, I swear. But now you are free. You are saved."

"Saved? From whom?" She pushes me away and turns to leave. "Go home, Kaspar. Your sister wants a word."

I watch as she slips into the shadows. Out on the water, in the rippling moonlight, is the sea creature. Did she observe our exchange? I walk home, wanting nothing more to do with mermaids or ungrateful widows.

I find the door to the rectory open to the night air.

The house is empty, the fire in the hearth has gone cold. Where the hell is everyone? I call out for my sister, my father, my pinheaded brother. No reply comes.

I cross the yard and enter the church, calling their names. The first thing I see are the bones scattered on the floor. Our sacred sea monster has been vandalized. A few pieces still hang on the wall, but the remainder of the skeleton lies in pieces on the flagstones of the chancel. There is a mouse darting among the broken fragments.

That's when I see father. Flat before the dais, and as still as stone. It's as if he's thrown himself to the floor, seeking mercy from the Almighty.

"Father, what's wrong? Why are you on the floor?"

I do not see the blood until I step up into the chancel. A great puddle of it on the cold slab, glistening and still growing. Red lines trace the grout of the flagstones. His head is not there. The stump of neck is an obscene display of gristle and bone, his lifeblood dribbling out from the thick arteries.

The brandy in my stomach curdles and comes back up. On my knees, I wretch and cough in a greasy sweat. I am brainless for a long moment, unable to comprehend the thing lying on the floor behind me. My first fevered thought is to blame the mermaid. That she has somehow slithered her way into the church to murder our father. But that is ludicrous.

It isn't until I hear the screaming that my shattered brain clicks upon the true culprit. The screams come from outside, and from every house. Shrieks of bald terror and calamities of violence. I hear names among the screams, pleas to stop whatever is happening.

*Lilja, no!*

*Heloise, stop!*

*No, Miriam! For the love of God, stop!*

*Bryndis, no! NO!*

That last voice. Pip. I stagger outside, looking for my brother. I hear him cry out once more, somewhere on the far side of the church. I lurch around the stone wall to the yard, but there is no Pip there. No Bryndis.

Bryndis.

Could our sister really have done this wickedness to Father? Bryndis is no fainting flower, but she is gentle with all living things. I can no more picture her speaking a harsh word to Father, let alone docking his head from his neck. It is too nightmarish to consider, and yet some twinge in my belly tells me it is true.

I call out for my brother, but immediately shut my mouth when shadows pass over the wall of the church. At the sound of footfalls in the lane, I hide behind a tombstone and make myself very small. As much as I cannot stop trembling, I force myself to peek out from behind the stone. The village daughters emerge from their cottages and hovels and into the streets. The tools in their hands drip with blood, the metal clotted with scraps of hairy scalp.

I run, scuttling away as quietly as I can. Searching for Pip but steering clear of the women now stalking through town. Sidling along walls and clinging to shadows, I make my way to the wharf. There I see a gangly creature with thin limbs and an oversize head, pacing up and down the stone pier. Pip, in a panic and veering dangerously close to where the wharf drops to the water below. On the moonlit ripples, I see the sailfin of the monster break the surface.

Bolting into the open, I snatch my brother away from the edge just as the water churns and boils. She surfaces in the sea foam, glaring with those double-lidded eyes as I drag Pip to safety.

Pip is ragged with tears. He sputters and babbles, making no sense. The only word I can decipher is our sister's name. Did he witness our father's murder? Did he watch the desecration of his body?

I pull him close to stifle his trembling. His runny nose dampens my collar as he shrinks into a shivering kitten. His voice hitches into a single question, repeated over and over.

Why?

When the first of the village girls steps into view, I clamp a hand over his mouth to silence him.

They make their way to the pier in a silent procession. Their bare feet on the cobblestones are painted red. Every daughter of our little hamlet passes by the shadow where Pip and I squat in terror. Every unmarried girl, every widow.

Pip buckles and goes into a fit when he sees what they are carrying in their clenched fists. I cannot hold him still with my ruined hand and he turns, seeing the horror in full. He sees the husks dripping gore along the stones. Heloise clutches her father's severed head by the beard, Sabine holds Ulric's noggin by one large ear. Father's head is gripped at the scalp by our sister. I see Agnet stride past with Gunther's head tucked under one arm like a gourd harvested from a garden.

Pip goes limp, fainting in terror. He slips through my useless hands like an eel. I want to scream, but my mouth is chalk and will make no sound. All I can do is watch the procession file out onto the pier where the mermaid glides across the bay. She is waiting for them.

A plop and a splash. The first head is tossed in. Then another and another, until the decapitated heads of all the men are pitched into the harbor in some pagan tribute to the sea goddess.

I unstick my tongue and hiss at my brother. "Pip, wake up. We have to get out of here."

There is no reply. My hands are empty. Pip is gone.

Distracted by the horrific ceremony on the pier, I do not notice him crawling away. There he squats, rocking back and forth with his head in his hands. Less than a yard from the water's edge. Vulnerable.

The sea erupts in a volcano of spray and saltwater. The mermaid bursts forth like the deity of some time before man ever was. Webbed fingers snatch Pip by the hair and pull him under the waves before he can even cry out. One of his tattered shoes clatters on the stone. The rest of my brother is gone.

I bury my face in my hands, telling myself that this is all a nightmare, a dream that I will soon wake from. The cry of the gulls fills the silence, along with the gentle wash of the surf on the beach. And beneath that everyday, mundane sound, I swear to God I hear a voice singing in a strange tongue. It is the most sublime thing I have ever heard.

# 19

MOTHER WAS A gifted storyteller. Every night, she would gather us close in the tallow light and tell us a story before bed. There were stories about knights finding enchanted swords or princesses escaping a witch's dungeon. Some were romances where the lovers were kept apart by wars or petty gods, but always united at the end and happily wed. Sometimes even death could not keep the lovers apart.

Mother had a knack for weaving her stories to a fevered pitch that left us breathless in fright and cowering under her skirts. And yet, no matter how dire the turns of the story, mother always thrilled us with twists and surprises, always, always stitching her stories closed with a happy knot. The downtrodden were lifted to glory, the underling stableboy made a knight by his king. The monster was defeated, the hero rewarded for her bravery with some fabled treasure.

Pip, being the youngest, would nestle in mother's lap like a bird and listen in holy rapture as she spun her tales.

When mother disappeared, it was the stories that we missed most, I think. Pip had the hardest time accepting that, not only was mother gone, but so too were her fairy tales. At bedtime, he would light the candle and wait for mother to come, refusing to bed down until he had a story. Bryndis tried to pacify him, but her stories came out confusing and contradictory. I tried my hand at spinning yarns, but I would get lost in the plot and could never thread my way to the happy ending.

When Pip wailed for mother and her stories, the mewling grated horribly on Father's nerves. One night, one dark and stormy night, it proved too much. Pip had worked himself into a lather, and although scolded by Father to stop, he could not. The mewling echoed through the room and Father went at him, striking him with blow after blow until blood shot from Pip's ears. I believe he would have killed our brother if Bryndis and I hadn't pulled him away. Pip was never the same after that. Some portion of his brain was knocked loose and rolled under the bed, never to be seen again.

I remember this now, as the waves close over Pip's terrified face, and he disappears into the depths. If the water blooms red with his blood, I do not see it. It ripples black, then silver.

There is a hand on my shoulder. I don't need to lift my head to know it's her.

"Come, Kaspar," she says. "It's time."

Agnet holds out her slender hand. I take it and she pulls me up.

"Time for what?"

"You are the last man." Agnet leads me by the hand to the pier. There is something wrong with her neck. "That makes you king now."

I try to laugh but cannot. I can taste saltwater in my mouth.

"King of what? A village of rotting octopus?"

Framed in the silvery light are three strange slits running along Agnet's neck. They throb and pulsate, and I realize these are gills. Agnet is not singular in this. My sister sports them too, along with Sabine. All of them have gills.

I do not want this, whatever it is. I try to pull away, but Agnet's grip is too strong. The bones of my leprous hand break under her iron grasp.

"You are lord of the realm now, Kaspar. Hero and king to a village of women. Doesn't that make you happy?"

They march me down to the end where the stone pier drops away into the sea. I see their hands, pushing and dragging me along, are strangely webbed between the fingers.

"Don't do this, Agnet. Please."

I am reduced to begging, to bargaining for my life, but I have nothing to barter with.

"Don't beg, Kaspar. It's unkingly."

There is a coronet in Agnet's hand. The same crown of wriggling starfish that Pip made for me. She places it on my head, and I feel the creatures squirm over my scalp.

"God save the King," she says sweetly.

The water ripples. The mermaid is nigh. Is this what Hagar meant when she spoke of the luremaid marking me for a reason? My reward, my doom.

"She's the queen? Is that it?"

Agnet smiles. One last glimpse at the gap in her teeth. "Oh, she's much more than that."

The water churns as her barbed fin cuts through the slash of moonlight. The sea monster grows impatient.

"A kiss, Agnet? Please?"

Her smile goes away. "She has all your kisses, Kaspar. Go fetch them."

They throw me in. My reign is short.

The water is cold, and it thrums heavily in my ears. But there is no pain, no sharp teeth tearing my limbs apart. She is here, circling me in the depths, but she is gentle. She pulls me down, down to the waving kelp and sandy floor of the sea.

There is a procession marching across the seabed. Single file, the dead men trod over seashells and the broken ribs of sunken ships. Heads down, but I recognize each one. Old Ulric and tall Lothar. Gunther the Brave and my father. Pip. The men of the village plod silently in martial order, lockstep to some destination that I cannot see.

Perhaps there is no destination. Maybe we simply march and march and march.

The mermaid sets me down at my place at the end of the line. Right behind Pip. I want him to turn and look at me, but he does not. All I see is the back of his misshapen head.

Onward, we march.

# ACKNOWLEDGMENTS

Where do books come from? Who knows? How are books made? Well, there's a support team whose efforts sometimes get overlooked in the hoopla about the finished product. Here's a few that helped bring this little story to life. Without them, this project would have sunk to the bottom of the salty ocean.

First and always, thanks to Monique for her constant support, wisdom and love throughout. Even when I'm talking nonsense. Also to Ruby and Ginger, who keep me humble and laughing.

Thanks to Matt Blairstone who guides the ship at Tenebrous Press for believing in this weird tale and bringing it into the Tenebrous armada of weird fiction. Double thanks for his amazing cover!

Barrels of thanks go to editor Alex Woodroe for her insights and expert guidance at making the story the best it could be. Her enthusiasm for storytelling is infectious in the best possible way. Also, full credit goes to Alex for coining the term "luremaid," which hit the bullseye.

Thanks to artist Kelly Williams for his jaw-dropping interior art. This is as close as I'll ever get to collaborating on a graphic novel.

A huge thanks to Catherine McCarthy for her help in shaping the story, and for her friendship and support in this wacky writing biz. Boatloads of thanks to Laurel Hightower for her notes and constant inspiration. And sincere appreciation to Eric LaRocca for his kind words on this weirdo novella.

Thanks to author Brian Francis for his constant support

and sympathetic ear over many a beer-and-bitch session. You are loved.

To Mom, for always believing. And to the horror community at large for being so welcoming. And not just to me, but to everyone who loves this genre. Seeing you all share your victories, your setbacks, and support for one another is like oxygen to me.

# ABOUT THE AUTHOR:

**Tim McGregor** is the author of *Hearts Strange and Dreadful*, the *Spookshow* series, and a handful of other titles. *Taboo in Four Colors* comes out in November. Tim lives in Toronto with his wife, two kids, and one spiteful ghost. He can be reached at timmcgregorauthor.com

## ABOUT THE ARTIST:

**Kelly Williams** draws stuff. He's online at treebeerdstuff.com.

# CONTENT WARNINGS

**LURE** contains scenes that deal with:
*Domestic violence and misogyny
*Implied suicide

Please be advised.

More information at
www.tenebrouspress.com

# ABOUT TENEBROUS PRESS

Tenebrous Press was conceived in the Plague Year 2020 and unleashed, howling and feral, in spring 2021 to deliver the finest in transgressive, progressive Horror from diverse and unsung voices around the world.

We welcome the esoteric; the unorthodox; the finest in New Weird Horror.

### FIND OUT MORE:
www.tenebrouspress.com
Twitter: @TenebrousPress

# NEW WEIRD HORROR

TENEBROUS

10p

PRESS

CPSIA information can be obtained
at www.ICGtesting.com
Printed in the USA
BVHW040100250722
642923BV00001B/1